The Curious Cat Spy Club

Book Two
The Mystery of the Zorse's Mask

Linda Joy Singleton

Albert Whitman & Company
Chicago, Illinois

To my husband, David, who loves horses and
helped me search for a real zorse

Library of Congress Cataloging-in-Publication data
is on file with the publisher.

Text copyright © 2015 by Linda Joy Singleton
Cover illustration copyright © 2015 by Kristi Valiant
Interior illustrations and hand lettering by Jordan Kost
Published in 2015 by Albert Whitman & Company
ISBN 978-0-8075-1378-1

Printed in the United States of America
10 9 8 7 6 5 4 3 2 1 LB 20 19 18 17 16 15

Design by Jordan Kost and Ellen Kokontis

For more information about Albert Whitman & Company,
visit our web site at www.albertwhitman.com.

Contents

- Chapter 1 -
Spy Games

I snap steel handcuffs on my captive's wrists. "You will *not* escape."

"I will," he says with no fear. But he should be afraid. His legs are tied to a chair and his arms are cuffed behind his back. We're in a shack in the woods, so if he screams, only wild animals will hear—and they won't help.

"Try to get out. I dare you."

He smiles. "According to my calculations, I'll be free in seven and a half minutes."

"You'll never break loose from the cuffs without this." I wave a silver lock pick in his face, then place it on the table—far out of reach.

With a click of the overhead light, I plunge the

room into darkness.

I leave and lock the door.

I'm grinning as I step outside the Skunk Shack. It's a cloudy day with a crisp spring breeze that flings my hair across my face. I push my hair back and bend over a basket where three kittens curl together, sleeping. I pet the orange kitten I named Honey. She stirs with a flick of her stubby tail, then drifts back to sleep.

I walk over to Becca, who's perched on our favorite stump that is as wide and high as a table. Her glitter-striped sneakers dangle over the prickly weeds. She taps her heels rhythmically against the stump like there's a song in her head.

"How'd it go, Kelsey?" Becca asks. "Is he locked up?"

"Snug as a bug in a jar," I say proudly. "No way can he get loose."

"You hope," she teases.

"I know." My title in our club is Spy Tactic Specialist—and I'm good at it. Let the spy games begin!

"I have something for you." I dig into my pocket for a folded piece of paper and hold it out to Becca. "A letter."

Her dark eyes widen in surprise. "You've never written to me before."

"Never had a reason," I say in a hushed tone, a twig snapping beneath my foot. "This letter reveals a *big* secret."

Becca stops tapping her heels against the stump as she leans closer to me.

"From your collection?"

I nod. Becca is the only person who knows I collect secrets the way other girls collect shoes. Most of my secrets come from being observant—like when I saw Trever Auslin destroy a school textbook. I don't tattle or gossip. Instead, this became secret twenty-seven in my notebook of secrets. No one has ever seen my notebook—not even Becca.

"Here." I hold out the letter. But as Becca reaches for it, I pull it away. "No. I've changed my mind."

I rip the letter into pieces that float to the ground like tiny parachutes.

"*Kelsey!*" Becca exclaims. "I can't believe you did that!"

"Believe it." I press my lips together firmly.

"But I wanted to read it."

"So read it." I smile. "Put the letter back together, girl sleuth. Here's some tape."

"Oh." Becca nods in understanding as she takes the tape. "This is a spy lesson, like what our captive, Leo, is getting."

"Good deduction." I nod. "Imagine you're trailing a suspect. He sits on a park bench and a woman sits beside him. They act like they don't know each other, but the woman sneaks a note to the suspect. After she leaves, he reads the note, rips it, and tosses the pieces into a trash can. Your challenge is to put the letter back together. Make sure all the pieces fit perfectly before taping them." I look at my wristwatch. "You have ten minutes."

Becca jumps off the stump and chases after the scraps of paper, a few dancing away from her on the wind.

I squat beside the kittens to watch the show. While Becca captures paper, I listen for sounds from inside the shack. Leo should have chair-hobbled to the table by now. If he's really flexible, he'll wiggle his feet through his arms so his cuffed hands are in front of instead of behind his back. I would love to watch, but Leo insisted on working in the dark to make the spy lesson more challenging.

So I cuddle with Honey while Becca chases after wind-blown paper. The pieces of paper swirl out of her reach like fluttering moths. As she grabs for a tiny piece, the wind steals it away and she stumbles to the ground. Instead of getting mad or quitting, she jumps back up, laughing. Even dusted in dirt, with hair falling out of her ponytail, she looks chic.

Lately, I've started wearing my hair in a ponytail too. It's not pink-streaked and curly black like Becca's; it's plain brown and too straight. Becca's the coolest girl I know, and so creative, she designs her own wild-animal-print outfits. She's in my science class at school, but we didn't become friends until I helped catch her runaway zorse (an animal that is part zebra, part horse). When we found kittens trapped in a dumpster, Leo joined in the rescue, which led to a secret club and three secret kittens.

Well, just two kittens after today.

Leo is taking his calico kitten home. He can finally have a cat because his allergic dad moved out. Not a happy reason, although Leo says his parents are happier apart. Leo is so lucky that he can keep his kitten. Becca can't because her mom already fosters too many cats. I can't because I live in a cramped apartment with two adults and four kids. But Dad will hear about a new job today, which could mean moving into a house where we can have pets.

"Got it!" Becca announces and holds up a scrap of paper.

I glance at my watch. "Three minutes left."

"I can do it!" Becca carries the tape and papers over to the stump, spreading out the scraps like puzzle pieces.

While I watch her, I think how much I love being in the Curious Cat Spy Club. Becca, Leo, and I created the CCSC to care for our three kittens, but now our goal is to help all animals—and solve mysteries. Last week we unmasked a pet-napper, and we have two more mysteries to solve: Why did someone leave a broken grandfather clock in the Skunk Shack? What really happened to Zed the Zorse?

I feel sick whenever I think of Zed's ugly scars. The sweet zebra-horse has been at Wild Oaks Sanctuary, run by Becca's mother, for over six months. No one knows where he came from, but he has scars from being beaten. Becca thinks he ran away from an abusive owner. She freaked out last week after a man called, saying he's the owner and wants Zed back. But the man didn't leave his name or number and hasn't shown up. Becca is relieved because she loves Zed and hopes he can stay at Wild Oaks forever.

I glance at my watch. "Two minutes."

"But I'm missing a piece!" Becca finally finds the paper stuck to the bottom of her sneaker.

She finishes the challenge with thirty-five seconds to spare.

"Great work!" I pat her shoulder.

Becca doesn't answer because she's already reading the taped letter.

What will she think of the secret I revealed? I've learned lots of secrets because I'm so quiet that people don't notice me. It wouldn't be right to reveal someone else's secret to Becca though, so I shared something terrible I did when I was five. I got mad at my mom and hid so well no one could find me, then I fell asleep. I didn't know everyone was looking for me until I woke up hours later and saw the police car.

"Wow." Becca looks up from the letter. "You must be really good at hiding."

"No one beats me at hide-and-seek. But I still feel guilty for what I did," I add more seriously. "When I saw my parents talking to a policeman, I was scared I'd get into trouble, so I made up a story about being kidnapped. I don't know if my parents believed me, but I felt guilty for lying to them. I've never told anyone the truth."

"Until now." Becca squeezes my hand. "I won't tell anyone—not ever. Thanks for trusting me with your secret." She tilts her head toward the Skunk Shack. "Should we go free Leo?"

"According to his calculations, he should have unlocked the handcuffs by now," I say lightly.

"He won't escape that easily," Becca says.

I chuckle. "He's a whiz with robots but not handcuffs."

"Poor guy needs rescuing." Becca playfully tugs my arm. "Come on. Let's help him."

We enter the shack, which is dark until I turn on the lamp. "Game over, Leo," I call as light brightens the room.

The chair I left him tied to is empty.

Leo is gone.

"Where is he?" Becca turns in a circle to look around our clubhouse.

I check under the table, behind the grandfather clock, and even inside a rusty metal cabinet too small for anyone to hide in.

"I don't understand." I twist my ponytail around my finger. "There's no way he could get out. The door was locked. We would have seen if he'd come outside."

"He must have crawled through the window," Becca says with a gesture toward the only window in the clubhouse, which is darkened by shutters.

"Impossible. The shutters are locked from the outside."

"Look!" Becca points to the table.

I follow her gaze to the pair of shiny silver handcuffs. Grabbing them, I check to see if they're broken. But they look as good as when they arrived in the mail from Spy Guys.

"The lock pick is gone." I tuck the cuffs into my pocket. "Leo must have it. But where is he?"

"Turn around!"

I whirl at Leo's voice. He's standing in the doorway, grinning. His blond hair is swept back neatly, and there's not a speck of dirt on his white button-down, vest, or black slacks.

Becca shakes her head, puzzled. "How did you escape?"

"Utilizing strategy and logic," Leo says with a shrug. "I couldn't climb onto the table with handcuffs on. But the table is lopsided, so I tilted it until the lock pick slid into my hands. As I calculated, I had the handcuffs off within seven and a half minutes."

"But how did you get out of the room?" I demand. "We were outside the door. And the window shutters are locked."

"This lock pick you taught me to use is an efficient tool." He holds up my silver pick. "I used the flat end to pry off the window screen. I reached around to unlock the latch, then crawled outside and onto the roof. The hardest part was not laughing while Becca chased after those papers."

"You sneaky spy!" Becca accuses.

"I'll take that as a compliment." Leo bows.

"Great job, both of you," I say. "You've proven your spy skills."

"It was super fun," Becca says. She picks up an empty kitten food packet and tosses it in the trash. "We have to leave soon. Let's tuck the kittens inside for the night."

Leo grins as he scoops up his calico. "Lucky is coming home with me."

"Lucky you," I say enviously.

As Becca reaches the door, her cell phone rings.

She glances down at the screen and rolls her eyes. "It's my mother."

"Again?" I raise my brows.

"Mom probably found more chores for me. She could ask one of the volunteers, but no, she'd rather work me to death—sweep out the monkey cage, refill the rabbit feeders, pick up bird feathers. Wish I could ignore this…" Becca shrugs and answers.

She holds the phone to her ear, listening. Her lips pinch like she's biting back her temper. Suddenly she tenses. Her eyes go wide, and she clutches the phone with both hands. "No! You can't let him do that!"

Can't let who do what? I wonder, coming over to stand beside Becca. I want to give her a hug or say something soothing, but I have no idea what's wrong.

A touch on my hand makes me look up to find Leo standing beside me. His hand brushes mine as we wait.

"Mom, tell him no…Please don't let this happen," Becca pleads, close to tears. "Don't you even care that he could die?" Shaking her head, she shoves the phone into her pocket.

"Are you okay?" I ask.

"I am—but Zed won't be."

Leo lifts his brows. "The zorse is in trouble?"

"The worst." Becca scowls. "The man who claims to own him, the same man who probably beat him, wants him back."

"Oh no!" I gasp.

"If he hurt Zed once, he'll do it again," Becca says furiously. "He's coming to take Zed away in two days. And there's nothing we can do to stop him."

Chapter 2

Secret
Twenty-Nine

While the kittens chase each other around the dismantled grandfather clock, we pull our chairs close to the table.

"Tell us what your mom told you," I say to Becca.

"Don't leave any details out," Leo adds.

"Mom said his name is Caleb Hunter and he lives over a hundred miles away on a ranch in Nevada. His grandma owns Zed, but she's really sick and in a nursing home." Becca grabs a berry juice packet from our snack box and takes a sip. "On the night Zed disappeared, his grandma had a stroke and was rushed to the hospital in an ambulance. Caleb thinks the siren spooked Zed and that's why he broke out of his corral."

"How did Zed end up in California?" Leo asks, wrinkling his brow.

"No one knows. Everyone assumed he was dead until Caleb recognized Zed in an online news photo." Becca rubs her finger on a stain on the table, her dark eyes narrowing. "At least that's what he told Mom."

"You don't believe him?" I ask, surprised.

"Zed has been with us for over six months. His photo was posted all over the Internet and even on TV news. If Caleb Hunter cared so much for Zed, why didn't he find him sooner? I won't let that man have Zed," she says with the fierceness of a mother zorse protecting her foal.

"He has a legal right to take the zorse," Leo points out in his usual, practical tone.

"Doesn't Zed have any rights?" Becca argues. "You didn't see Zed when he came to stay at our sanctuary, but I did and my heart broke. One eye was swollen shut, his coat was matted with dried blood, and he had stripes of scars from being whipped. He looked like a wild beast, but we knew he was someone's pet because he was wearing a fancy fly mask. He let Mom and me touch him but trembled if a man came near, so I know it was a man who beat him."

"That doesn't mean it was Caleb," I put in, trying to be fair.

Becca purses her lips stubbornly. "He probably knows who did it."

"Not if Zed was hurt after he ran away," Leo points out.

"How do we know Caleb's grandma even owns Zed? He says Zed's real name is Domino Effect, which doesn't fit Zed at all. He could have made up the whole story about a sick grandma to get our sympathy, so we'll hand over Zed. What if he's scamming us so he can sell Zed for lots of money?"

"Easily verified. I'm on it," says Leo, our club Covert Technology Strategist. He taps quickly on his cell phone, then reports, "Caleb Hunter, age thirty-six, resides in Nevada, divorced, no kids, and works as a horse trainer for D. S. Ranch. His parents moved to Arizona, but his younger sister, Carol Hunter-Bowling, and grandmother are in Nevada. His grandmother, Eloise Hunter, resides at Golden Meadows Senior Care Home."

"Okay, so he's not lying." Becca crumples her juice packet, red juice squirting on her fingers. "But he still could be the brute who abused Zed. And since Mom won't protect Zed, it's up to me." Becca wipes her hands with a napkin, then holds them out imploringly to us. "Will you help me? Caleb's coming on Saturday and I could use your support."

"Nothing could keep me away," I say, placing my hand over hers.

"Me either," Leo adds his hand on ours.

We make sure the kittens have plenty of food and water, then leave the Skunk Shack. Becca only has a short hike down the hill to her wild-animal-sanctuary home, but Leo and I live a few miles away. Leo's kitten is snug in a pet carrier as Leo rolls off on his techno gyro-board (a speedy robotized skateboard that bends in the middle), and I walk the wooded trail back to my bike.

As I pedal home, I wonder how Zed got all the way from Nevada to California. It's amazing he survived. But his injuries are suspicious. He wasn't clawed by a bear or cougar; he was beaten by a human. Becca suspects Caleb, but I'm not so sure. If he hated the zorse enough to beat him, why drive over a hundred miles to get him? Sure, Zed is valuable, but he's a lot of work. He's stubborn and doesn't like to ride in the trailer, so traveling with him won't be easy.

Is Caleb Hunter a nice guy trying to reunite his

sick grandma with her favorite pet? Or is he a liar and a fraud?

I'll find out on Saturday.

My spokes whirl as I coast into small-town Sun Flower, spinning my thoughts in a new direction. Soon I'll know if Dad got the job at the bakery where he interviewed last week. Working at a bakery is the most perfect job in the world for him. And he's so talented, how could anyone not want to hire him? When Dad bakes, he's like a sculptor creating a masterpiece. Mom teases that he should change his name to "More" because that's what people say after they taste his cookies, cakes, and homemade bread.

I roll up to my apartment complex, lock my bike in the rack, and sniff the air for a whiff of celebratory dessert. When Dad bakes, he opens all the windows so yummy smells sweeten the air. In our old neighborhood, people found excuses to stop by.

As I walk up the stairs, I don't smell anything baking. I unlock the front door and cautiously peek inside the living room. The TV is off and no one sits at the computer. I check the kitchen, and it's empty too.

Voices murmur from down the hall, so I slip into

spy mode and investigate. My twin older sisters, Kiana and Kenya, share the first room. I don't hear them, so I check inside and see the usual mess— beds unmade and clothes scattered on the carpet. My sisters are probably hanging with their friends. I peek into my brother's room too. Kyle is a neat freak, so everything is where it belongs, from the pillows on his bed to the pens on his computer desk. All that's missing is Kyle.

Voices rise then fall in my parents' room.

I creep over to their door to listen.

"—was so sure," Dad says with a groan.

"The next one will be even better," Mom encourages, but her voice is heavy with disappointment.

"If there's a next one," he adds grimly.

Oh no! I realize Dad didn't get the job. Last time this happened, he paced the apartment like a caged animal for days and growled if anyone mentioned the word *job*. No surprise my siblings found somewhere else to be.

"You'll find another job," Mom says confidently.

"Not in the food industry and"—he lowers his voice, so I miss a few words—"have to move to a big city."

"I hope not." Mom sighs. "Sun Flower is our home. I don't want to leave."

"I like it here too, but I can't get a job, and your job at the florist is only part-time. Moving may be our only option."

"I know..." She sighs again. "But moving away will be hard on the kids. Let's keep this a secret until we know for sure. No reason to worry them."

"I'll do the worrying—it's the one job I can't be fired from," Dad adds bitterly. Then I hear the sound of footsteps.

"Drats," I mutter. He's coming my way.

I rush down the hall and duck into my room. Breathing hard, I sprawl out on my bed and stare up at the ceiling. The apartment walls are thin, so I can hear Dad stomp down the hall into the kitchen and slam the cupboards. He must be "vent-cooking," a word my sisters came up with to describe the pots and pans banging when he's in a bad mood while making dinner. My sisters say it's therapeutic. I say it's noisy, so I put in earbuds and listen to my iPod while I catch up on my homework.

It's hard not to think about the secret I just overheard. But factoring equations distracts me from worrying. By the time I join my family for dinner, Dad has calmed down enough to smile. He even makes a pun about what a ghost calls spaghetti

—spookghetti—and it feels good to laugh.

Before I go to bed that night, I take out my notebook from the hidden drawer in my wooden chest and flip open to a new page.

Secret twenty-nine—If Dad doesn't find a job, we'll have to move. Losing our house was bad enough, but leaving Sun Flower would be worse. *No more biking over to Gran's house to visit her and our dog, Handsome. I'll be the new girl at a new school where I don't know anyone. No CCSC, Skunk Shack, secret kittens, or Leo or Becca.*

As I bike to school the next morning, I brainstorm ways to stay in Sun Flower. It would be cool if I could win a lottery and hand over a huge check to my parents. While I earn some money for the CCSC Kitten Care Fund by returning lost pets, I'm too young to get a job or even enter a lottery. How can I help my family?

I don't have any ideas, but Leo and Becca may.

We can make it a CCSC project.

Smiling, I coast through the gates into Helen Corning Middle School and lock up my bike.

Becca is in my science class. I slip into the seat behind her, but she doesn't turn around to talk to me because we're keeping our club a secret to protect the kittens. One of her three Sparkler group friends, Chloe, sits across from her, and they're always whispering or covert texting. Becca is close enough to touch, but it's like she's far away on a distant planet, speaking a language only Sparklers understand.

I'll have to wait till later to talk to her. But I might be able to talk to Leo at lunch. He always sits alone, designing robots on his tablet. I eat with friends from my old neighborhood, Ann Marie and Tori. They're talkative and obsessed with sports, which is cool because I hear all the gossip about the jocks.

But I hesitate as I enter the noisy cafeteria, clutching my sack lunch and water bottle to my chest. I stare at the back of the room, where hoop players crowd one end of a long table. At the other end, Leo Polanski sits alone.

His blond hair falls across his face as he eats a pita sandwich while writing on his tablet. He's an island of Leo-ness, isolated and unaware that a sea of life swims around him. He doesn't even realize how alone he is, which makes it worse, and I feel sorry for him.

So I make a decision.

Today I'll sit with Leo.

He's my friend, and I don't care if anyone knows. He shouldn't be so alone.

First I stop by the table where I usually sit with Ann Marie and Tori. They're best friends but sound like worst enemies as they argue over a referee's call at a soccer game. I tell them I'm going to sit with another friend and they're cool with it.

Sucking in a deep breath, I start for Leo's table.

I'm halfway there when someone calls my name.

Turning, I scan the crowd until I spot Becca waving from the Sparkler table. I swivel around to see who she's waving to—then I realize it's me. Seriously, what's she doing? I mean, she's the one who suggested we pretend not to know each other at school. So why is she calling my name?

"Kelsey," she says again, weaving through tables to stand beside me.

I cover my mouth and whisper, "You're totally blowing our secret."

"This doesn't have anything to do with CCSC. Come on. You'll find out."

"But keeping our friendship a secret was *your* idea."

"You sit behind me in science. It's not weird for me to talk to you."

"Well...yeah," I say, pleased but puzzled.

"Come with me." Becca hooks her arm through mine. "Over to my table."

I look at her suspiciously. Is this some kind of joke?

"No joke," she says as if reading my mind. "I've talked with the girls and they want you to join us."

"You mean, I can sit with the Sparklers?"

"Not just sit." Becca's grin widens. "The Sparklers need your help."

- Chapter 3 -
Sparkling!

It's like one of my dreams turned into real life—the dream where I'm a famous celebrity and the whole world loves me. Fans beg me to take a selfie with them, and every word I say is clever and hilarious. Best of all, in this dream, Becca and I are best friends.

I pinch myself to make sure I'm not dreaming.

Ouch. Wide-awake.

I glance regretfully at lonely Leo. I'll sit with him tomorrow.

The short walk to the Sparkler table is the longest walk I've ever taken. I can't help but worry that this is a trick and I'll end up humiliated. It happens in teen movies all the time. But Becca would never be a mean girl.

Why would the Sparklers want me to hang out with them? I'm so quiet that most kids—sometimes even teachers—don't remember my name. I'm a T-shirt and jeans girl, not a glittery diva. Sparkly isn't my style.

"Here's Kelsey," Becca says with a sweeping gesture toward me.

She introduces the three other girls to me, although I know who they are. They wear identical silver crescent-moon necklaces but are very different. Sophia has short, spiky brown hair, dimples, and three diamond studs in each ear. Model tall and graceful, Tyla wears black braids that are woven with strands of silver that make her silver-gray eyes shine like stars. And Chloe is adorably loud and curvy, with blue hair and big, jeweled glasses that would be dorky on anyone else.

"You look familiar," Chloe booms in a voice that cuts through cafeteria noises. She's the leader of the Sparklers.

"I sit near you in science."

"Oh yeah." She shrugs, her blue-glitter lashes fluttering. "Don't you love Ms. Grande? She's the coolest teacher and so pretty—like a princess from a Disney cartoon with her red, wavy hair down to her waist."

"Yeah, she's cool," I agree, trying not to laugh because I discovered Ms. Grande's secret on a blustery day when the wind whipped her hair off her head. Her princess hair is actually a wig.

Becca squeezes in between Chloe and Sophia, then scoots over to make room for me. "I'm so glad you're here," she says, hugging me.

But why did you invite me? I wonder as I stare uneasily at the dazzling girls around me. "It's cool to be with you...but I'm not really the Sparkler type."

"Why not?" Becca blinks as if surprised.

I can think of like a zillion reasons, but Becca is so sincere, I don't want to disappoint her. So I think of this as a spy lesson, like when Leo escaped handcuffs and Becca pieced together the paper secret. My covert mission is to blend in like a chameleon, to think, talk, and act sparkly.

Not an easy challenge. To start off with, the other girls have hot food trays. I'm the only brown bagger at the table.

"Becca didn't tell us much about you," Chloe says as she spreads butter thick on her biscuit.

"Not much to tell." I open my water bottle and take a sip.

"She just doesn't want to brag," Becca says with a pat on my shoulder. "Kelsey is really smart, loves reading and games, and is great with animals."

I shine under Becca's praise and feel less awkward. "I'm not *that* smart, but my grades are okay."

"Better than okay—like straight *A*s," Becca says proudly. "It's because she works really hard at everything."

"Except her appearance." Tyla sweeps a critical look over me and plucks at my green shirt. "Where did you buy this?"

"I don't remember. I've had it forever," I say, not wanting to admit it's a hand-me-down from my sisters.

"Ignore the fashion snob." Becca smooths her fingers across her white tiger-striped jacket. "You should hear what Tyla says about my style. You're amazing the way you are, and you'll love helping us with our project. Some kids think we're all about sparkly clothes, but that's just for fun. We work on fund-raisers for our community and school. Last month, we had a car wash to earn money for the drama club."

"Theater rocks," Sophia pipes up in her cute, little-girl voice.

"Sophia is an actress," Chloe adds proudly.

"I'm in the drama club, and our next play is *The Lion King*. I'm going to be Nala."

"Congratulations!" I say, giving her a high five. "Great role."

"But it won't leave her much time for Sparkler projects." Chloe leans forward, taking back her role of leader. "In a few weeks, we're running a booth at the Humane Society Fund-Raiser."

"Yeah, Becca says it'll help lots of homeless animals get adopted." I think of the dogs, cats, rabbits, goats, and other animals at Wild Oaks Animal Sanctuary. "I want to help out too."

"Becca told us you would," Chloe says. "And we can really use your help. Start by helping us come up with an idea for our booth. Becca says you're creative, so think of something amazing."

Me? I know nothing about creating booths. Still, they're all looking at me eagerly, so I smile.

Chloe stabs a chicken strip with her fork. "All the best ideas have been done to death, like a dunking booth, balloon popping, and face painting."

"I still think we should do face painting again,"

Tyla says with a pout. "It was super popular last year."

"Except we lost money because the makeup cost more than what we made." Chloe gives Tyla an accusing look.

"Did you want to use crap cosmetics?" Tyla argues.

I listen with interest, not so much to their words but to their narrowed eyes, pressed lips, and sharp tones. Clearly, all is not rainbows and glitter with the Sparklers.

While their talk shifts from booth plans to favorite TV shows, I set my brown bag on the table and take out my triple-layered turkey, veggie, and cranberry sauce sandwich on sourdough, and four cinnamon caramel chip cookies.

"Those cookies smell yummy," Chloe says, sniffing.

"My dad's a whiz in the kitchen," I say. "He made the cookies."

"Can I have one?" Chloe asks.

"Sure." I hand her and her friends a cookie each. Dad's cookies brought me and Becca together, and now they're helping me win over her friends.

"Kelsey, you didn't keep one for yourself," Becca points out, then splits hers in half and we share.

Chloe downs her cookie in two bites. "Amazing!" she says, licking her lips. "I wasn't sure about inviting you to help with the booth project, but you're cool."

"Told you so," Becca says, slipping her arm around me.

"You sure did," Chloe says then turns to me. "We can't make you a Sparkler, but we can give you something to wear while you're helping with our project. You'll have to return it when the fundraiser is over, but until then, everyone will treat you like you're one of us."

She digs into her backpack and pulls out a tiny silver charm on a necklace, identical to the necklaces each of them is wearing.

A sparkling star perched on a crescent moon.

I'm temporarily a Sparkler.

- Chapter 4 -

Good-Bye, Zed

Saturday morning, I wake up with a bad feeling. Today Caleb Hunter comes to take Zed—unless we can stop him. If there's anything shady about Caleb, we'll find out. Then it'll be war—the CCSC against CH.

When I get to Becca's two-story white farmhouse trimmed in yellow, her mother tells me she's gone to the pasture to catch Zed.

Mrs. Morales is an older version of Becca—same shiny, black curls, only shorter; long, black lashes; and full lips framed by an oval face. She's smiling as she steps down from the porch, but I notice shadows under her eyes, like she didn't sleep well.

"Kelsey, I'm so glad you're here," she says, giving

me a warm hug. "Becca is going to need friends today."

"Yeah," I say. "She really loves Zed."

"I do too, but she blames me." Mrs. Morales shakes her head wearily. "I don't want Zed to leave either, but legally I have to return him to his owner."

"I guess," I say uneasily.

"Becca thinks I'm being unfair, but I'm just doing my job. It's not easy running Wild Oaks alone." She clutches the stair rail like it's all that's holding her up. "I wish Becca could understand that giving up Zed is hard on me too."

She looks at me like she's hoping I'll say I understand. I glance down at my sneakers. One of the laces is loose, so I bend down to tie it. When I stand up, the awkwardness is gone and Mrs. Morales is smiling again.

"Becca is in the back pasture." She points beyond the barn. "You girls have fun."

I hurry away, past the barn, to a fenced pasture. Unlatching the livestock gate, I make sure it's shut firmly behind me. I spot Becca by a bathtub that's been converted to a water trough. Dust swirls around my sneakers as I cross the pasture. Becca has her back to me as she holds out her hand to

Zed, trying to bribe him with oats. But Zed isn't having any of it.

"Come on, Zed," Becca coos. Her other hand dangles a rope behind her back. "You know you want the yummy oats."

Zed snorts and stomps a hoof.

"You'll have to try harder," I say.

"Maybe I'll let Caleb Hunter catch him," Becca grumbles. "Zed's stubborn. He can't be forced to do anything—you have to win his trust. It took a month before he'd let me ride him."

"It would be cool to ride him," I say.

"He likes you, so he might let you on his back. You can try when I catch him." She flings the lassoed rope toward Zed's neck, but he jerks away and she misses.

"If you catch him," I tease as Zed prances just out of reach.

"Ornery zorse," Becca mutters. "Did you know that a zorse is three times stronger than a horse? Last week while I was in school, he broke into the vegetable garden and refused to leave. One of our volunteers, Hank, couldn't catch Zed. By the time Mom got there to coax Zed out, he'd eaten a bunch of tomatoes and was chomping carrots. It's impossible for a man to get near him."

"Unless it's the man who used to own him," I say, then wish I hadn't when I see the pained look on Becca's face. "I'm sorry, Becca."

"It's not your fault. I was stupid to get attached." She tosses her dark ponytail over her shoulder. "I knew his owner might come for him. But as the weeks...months...went by, I started thinking he could stay."

"Maybe if Caleb sees how much you love Zed, he'll let you keep him."

Becca grabs more oats and holds out her hand toward the zorse. "Even if he did, Mom wouldn't agree. She can't wait to get rid of Zed."

"I don't think that's how she feels. But at least Zed is going to a loving home. Caleb's grandma will be so happy to have him back."

Becca frowns. "But she may be dying. What happens to Zed when she's gone?"

"Caleb will probably take care of him," I guess.

"If he really is who he says," Becca says, trying to bribe Zed with oats. "Come on, boy. Come and get it."

"He's sniffing like he's interested. You almost have him." I speak quietly, so I won't startle Zed.

"Another step and you can—"

Zed rears back with a toss of his black mane, flashing big teeth like he's grinning.

"Get over here, you stubborn brat!" Becca snaps.

"It's like he understands what's going on," I say.

"Oh, he does. Animals can read body language and sense moods. Zed usually comes right up to me." Her voice cracks. "I don't want him to leave." Oats spill from her fingers as she drops the lead rope and sinks to the ground. She covers her face with her hands.

I squat down and slip my arm around her shoulder. Hooves thump as Zed clomps over to us. He nuzzles Becca's neck. She reaches up and folds her arms around his dark mane.

Hugging Zed, she whispers to me, "Kelsey, get the rope."

Slowly, I rise to my feet. When Zed isn't looking, I grab the rope.

"Sneak up behind him, then loop it around his neck," Becca says. "That's my boy. Good Zed," she coos into his ear.

Here goes nothing, I think.

I swing out with the rope, toss it around Zed's neck—and miss!

Becca is quick though and grabs the rope. She holds Zed's black mane firmly with one hand as she lassos him with the other.

"Got you!" Becca exclaims. Her eyes shine with triumph...and tears.

Becca leads Zed toward the house, then pauses. "I can't do this...I need some time alone with Zed first...to say good-bye. Tell Mom I'm putting Zed in a barn stall. Leo will probably be here soon. Wait with him on the porch...until that man comes."

I nod, feeling so bad for her.

As I near the house, I'm startled to see a guy in a western hat sitting on the porch swing beside Becca's mom. *Oh no! Caleb Hunter is already here*, I think—until I get close enough to see his face.

"Leo?" I ask in surprise. "Since when did you go cowboy?"

"You must be referring to my hat." He tips the tawny-brown hat that's twice the size of his head. "Do you like it?"

"Sure." I cover my mouth so I won't giggle. Who wears a western hat with a button-down shirt and a pocket protector? Only Leo.

"Kelsey, why is Becca taking Zed into the barn?" Mrs. Morales frowns as she steps off the bench swing and points across the driveway. "I told her to bring him here."

"She's putting him in a stall so he's easy to catch and—" I hesitate. "To say good-bye."

"Oh." Mrs. Morales turns away but not before I see tears in her eyes.

A rumble vibrates the ground. I look up toward the front gate as a white truck pulling a large metallic-blue horse trailer drives through the gate. Gravel spits from the tires as the truck pulls up in front of the house. The driver is shadowed behind a tinted window, so I can't see his face until he comes to a stop and steps out onto the driveway.

Leo may think he looks like a cowboy in the wide-brimmed hat, but this muscular guy in polished leather boots, jeans, and a studded western shirt is the for-real thing. Caleb Hunter has a rugged face, smiling brown eyes, and a swath of sun-streaked brown hair across his tanned forehead.

Becca's mom hurries off the porch to meet him, her hand outstretched.

"Mr. Hunter?" They shake hands. "I'm Renee Morales."

"Pleasure to meet you, ma'am."

"No need to be formal," she says. "Call me Renee."

"Lovely name for a lovely lady," he says with a smile so warm that I wonder if he's flirting with Becca's mom.

Leo and I wait on the porch. He nudges me. "Can you hear what they're saying?"

"Mrs. Morales just said she hopes he had a good trip," I answer.

"I thought she said not to trip," Leo admits. "Your hearing is better than mine."

"Not really." I grin. "I'm lip-reading."

"What are they saying now?"

"Caleb isn't facing toward me, but Becca's mom is, and she said she's happy to reunite Zed with his family." I concentrate with both my eyes and ears. "She explained that we call the zorse Zed since we didn't know his name was Domino Effect."

"Zed is a more logical name for a zorse," says the very logical Leo. "Zed is the word most English-speaking countries—except the U.S.—use for the letter *Z*."

"*W, X, Y,* zed sounds weird," I say, focusing back on the driveway conversation. "Caleb gestured toward the trailer, but I can't see what he said. Becca's mom told him he'll need to sign papers before he takes Zed. She invited him into the house and offered him iced tea."

Leo licks his lips. "I like my iced tea with extra sugar."

"Lemon wedges are yummier...Oh!" I jump up, pointing across the driveway. "Here they come."

"The paperwork won't take long to fill out," Mrs. Morales says. She steps onto the wood-slat porch. "Also, I'll need to see proof of ownership."

Caleb Hunter holds out a folder and electronic tablet. "I got Grandma's certificate of registration — and something better right here on my tablet."

"I can't wait to see," Mrs. Morales says so warmly I wonder if she has a thing for cowboys. "I'll bet you're eager to see the zorse too."

"Sure am." He drawls out "sure" into two syllables. "Although it pains me knowing someone hurt him."

"He was near death when we took him in, but now he's healthy as a horse...I mean, a zorse." She glances over at the bench swing where Leo and I sit, all casual like we aren't eavesdropping.

"How could anyone beat such a gentle creature?" Caleb shakes his head, his voice thick with emotion. "I don't know what happened out in the wild. I'm just glad he's coming home, where he'll be treated like he deserves."

"My daughter has grown very fond of him too.

She's with him in the barn." Mrs. Morales gestures toward Leo and me. "These are her friends, Kelsey and Leo."

With a tip of his hat, Caleb Hunter runs his reply together like one word. "Gladtomeetyou."

Out of loyalty to Becca, I am not glad to meet him, but I'm curious. And the calculating look Leo gives him is sharp with curiosity too.

"My grandma raised Domino Effect—or you can call him Zed if you like," Caleb Hunter says. "She fussed over him something fierce, pampering and dressing him up in fancy doodads. She even allowed him in the house." Caleb gazes into Mrs. Morales's eyes. "Seeing him may give her the strength to hold on longer, which means a lot to me. I can't thank you enough for your kindness."

"Just doing my job," Mrs. Morales says, but she's blushing. "Let's go inside for the paperwork and iced tea."

"My pleasure," he says, then steps forward to open the door for Becca's mother before following her into the house.

"I want to see his proof too," Leo whispers to me.

"Exactly," I say. We hurry after the adults.

Minutes later, Leo and I sit at a wooden table in

the dining room, sipping lemony-perfect iced tea with Becca's mom and Caleb Hunter.

"These here are the legal documents for Domino," Caleb says as he hands over a slim blue folder. "He was a birthday gift to Grandma Ellie from Grandpa. When Grandpa died, Zed helped Grandma through her grieving. She loves that zorse like he's her child."

"He's easy to love." Mrs. Morales sighs as she glances through the folder.

"When Grandma was in the hospital, I made her a photo video of Zed from when he was just a foal," Caleb adds as he clicks on his electronic tablet. The background wallpaper shows a cowboy riding an appaloosa.

"That's you," I say to Caleb, pointing to the screen.

"I was riding before I could walk," he says proudly. "People come hundreds of miles so I can train their horses. Not to say I haven't had my share of tumbles. A mustang threw me so hard, I landed in barbed wire and got an infection that almost took my arm." He rolls up his left sleeve, and I wince at the jagged scars pale against his tanned skin.

"It looks painful." Mrs. Morales frowns with the

same softhearted expression I've seen on Becca. "Does it still hurt?"

"No," he says with a tough-guy shrug. And I swear, he flexes his muscles like he's a body builder.

He starts up the video of Zed's life, propping his tablet in the center of the table, so we all can see.

Zed was such a cute foal, with spindly legs and a gleam of mischief in his big, black eyes. His legs are ringed in black and white stripes, and his flank is darker than the splash of white he has now. In later photos, when Zed is fully grown, he wears a gaudy fly mask trimmed in jewels and his black tail is woven with pink ribbons.

"This here is Grandma, riding him in a parade," Caleb says.

A sun-wrinkled woman in black jeans and a leather vest sits confidently on a bejeweled pink saddle shiny enough to impress a Sparkler. Her western hat is pink too, and her long braid hangs like a silver mane over her shoulder. She looks a little like Caleb, with a similar straight nose and high cheekbones.

When the slide show ends, Caleb shuts the tablet and stands up from the table. "Thanks for your hospitality, but I need to pack up my zorse and be on my way."

Mrs. Morales hands him back the folder. "Everything looks in order. It's clear Zed belongs to your grandmother."

We file out of the house toward the barn.

"You probably already know this," Mrs. Morales says as the barn door slides open with a creak and ripe smell of hay, "but Zed shies away from men."

"Can't blame him for preferring women," Caleb adds with an appreciative look at Mrs. Morales. "But he'll remember me."

"He doesn't trailer well either," she adds.

"Don't I know that." Caleb chuckles. "Danged zorse has to be medicated before he'll get in a trailer. I brought a tranquilizer for the long ride home."

"Oh, I doubt you'll need that." Mrs. Morales shakes her black curls. "Becca can calm him down so he'll get into the trailer."

As we enter the barn, Zed peeks out over the door of the stall as Becca rests her arm around his neck.

"Becca, it's time," her mother says.

Becca presses her lips tight but doesn't argue. She won't look at her mother, only at Zed. I feel so bad because I wasn't able to help her keep Zed. But Caleb proved he has a right to take Zed. I'm sure

Zed will be happy with Caleb's grandmother.

"Come on, Zed." Becca wipes her eyes, then unlatches the stall. She leads Zed out by a rope.

But the zorse abruptly stops. His nostrils flare, and he lets out a harsh whinny. Caleb lunges forward to help Becca with Zed, but the zorse rears up.

"What's wrong, boy?" Becca tugs the lead rope.

Zed whinnies louder. He swishes his tail and refuses to budge.

"I was afraid of this," Caleb says. "Last time he saw me, I was getting into the ambulance that took Grandma Ellie away, which spooked him so much he took off and some scumbag beat him."

"Poor guy has been through a trauma," Mrs. Morales says.

"I should have taken better care of him," Caleb says regretfully.

"You'll have to be patient." Mrs. Morales approaches the zorse with her arm outstretched. "Calm down, Zed. Everything's okay. Caleb will take you back home."

Beside me, Leo mutters, "He'd rather stay with Becca."

"I know."

Zed's whinnies echo through the barn.

"I'm mighty sorry he's so much trouble," Caleb tells Mrs. Morales. "He never used to be so skittish. He's changed since running away and—" His eyes widen as he points to Zed. "Why isn't he wearing his mask?"

"What mask?" Becca's mother asks as she tries to shove Zed forward.

"His fly mask." Caleb frowns. "It's custom-made with bejeweled trim."

"He doesn't need one here." Mrs. Morales shakes her head. "We don't have a problem with flies."

"Grandpa gave Grandma the fly mask right before he died." Caleb frowns. "I know he was wearing it when you found him because I saw it in an online photo. So where is it now?"

- Chapter 5 -
Missing Mask

"I don't know anything about a fly mask," Mrs. Morales says while struggling to pull Zed out of the stall.

"Sure you do, Mom. Remember it was stuck to— stop it, Zed!" Becca cries out as Zed jerks sideways and the rope slips from her fingers. "Come back here, you ornery zorse!"

I start to chase after Zed, but Leo tugs me back. "You'll only be in the way."

He's right, which is so annoying. I move aside.

Caleb rushes forward to help, reaching to grab Zed, which freaks out the zorse again. Zed's hooves clatter as he shies away from his owner.

"Becca and I can get him into the trailer," Mrs. Morales offers.

"Mighty kind of you, ma'am." Caleb turns to Becca. "Now what were you saying about the fly mask?"

"Kind of busy here." Becca grits her teeth as she gives the zorse a powerful shove forward. "Zed, don't you dare kick! Watch out, Mom!"

Mrs. Morales jumps sideways to avoid Zed's hooves.

"Zed, stop freaking out and come with me now!" Becca pulls hard on the lead rope. But Zed is stronger and drags Becca back toward the stall.

Mrs. Morales looks over at Caleb. "I hate to ask, but could you go outside so we can calm Zed down?"

"Sure thing," Caleb says with a polite tip of his hat. "I'll open the trailer so you can walk him right in."

"That would be great. And take Leo and Kelsey with—hey, stop that!" she cries as Zed swishes her face with his black and white tail.

Being kicked out of the barn is better than being kicked by a zorse, so I follow Caleb through the door Leo holds open for us. As we leave the smell of hay and I breathe in crisp spring air, I can still hear stomping hooves.

Zed isn't leaving without a fight.

"He acts like he doesn't even know me." Caleb's voice is full of hurt. "He's afraid of me because some dirtbag abused him. If I knew who did it, I'd make sure he never touched another animal again."

"I want to find out too." I share a meaningful glance at Leo.

Could this be another mystery for the CCSC to solve?

"Unfortunately there's no way of knowing what happened." Caleb scuffs his pointy boot toe in the dirt. "But I blame myself for not being there to protect him. He'll calm down once he's with Grandma. But that's hours away."

Leo whispers in my ear, "He means miles. Distance is in miles, not hours."

I elbow Leo. "Shhh."

"It's going to be a long drive." Broad shoulders sagging, Caleb strides over to the horse trailer and unlatches the back door. Swinging it open, he goes inside.

"I feel sorry for him." I turn to Leo who is tilting his head with a "thinking" look.

"I wonder if there's any way to find out who abused Zed," Leo says.

"We could look for clues in the news articles," I

say. "Some of the people who saw him in the wild might have more information."

"Excellent suggestion." Leo taps his chin with his finger. "But first we need to determine the reliability of our key witness."

"Who?"

"Caleb Hunter." Leo gestures toward the trailer. "Is he being honest with us?"

"His photos prove his family owns Zed."

"Photos can be faked. Unlike you, I can separate my emotions from logic and consider all facts equally."

Sometimes I just want to smack Leo's brain right out of his head.

"I have looked at the facts," I retort. "Fact one: the photos, of course, which show him with Zed. Fact two: Caleb drove all the way here to return the zorse to his grandmother. Fact three: Caleb has legal ownership papers."

"You forgot fact four," Leo says. "Zed won't let Caleb near him."

"He probably won't let you touch him either," I point out. "He's afraid of all men because of the monster who hurt him."

Leo frowns. "If someone hurt him once, it could happen again."

I hear Caleb's footsteps thudding on the trailer floor. He must be getting the trailer ready for Zed. He's been friendly, helpful, and kind. But it would have been easier if he'd been a fraud so Becca could keep Zed.

There's a creak of the barn door opening. Becca and her mother come out with Zed. I don't know what magic they used on him, but he obediently trails after Becca, his head hanging down like he understands this is good-bye.

Becca says nothing as she walks Zed into the trailer. Her face is as easy to read as a book though, with lines of sorrow for this unhappy ending.

Caleb waits by the truck while Becca and her mother leave the trailer, and the metal door clangs shut.

Mrs. Morales turns to her daughter. "Honey, I'm so sorry," she says as she opens her arms to hug Becca. But Becca turns away. Without a word to her mother, she strides over to Leo and me.

"Want to go hang in your bedroom, Becca?" I ask gently, afraid she'll break down if she stays to watch the trailer drive away.

She looks at the horse trailer, then back to me. A tear drips down her cheek, to her Sparkler necklace.

"Come on." I take Becca's hand.

Leo moves to the other side of her. "We'll all go," he says.

We start for the house but only get a few steps before there's a shout behind us.

"Wait a minute, kids," Caleb hurries after us, holding his hat down with both hands when a gust of wind tries to snatch it away. He turns to Becca. "Would you mind getting the fly mask for me?"

"I'm not sure where it is." Becca wrinkles her brow. "But I'll go look."

"Mighty obliged," he says with a courteous tip of his hat. "It'll mean so much to Grandma to have both Zed and the fly mask back."

"It's been so long, I'm not sure I can find it." Becca frowns. "But I'll check the examination room."

"I'll help you look," I offer.

"We both will," says Leo.

Caleb waits by his truck while Becca leads us past the barn to a square, brown building. Inside it's bright from a skylight, with a large sink, a rectangular metal table, animal crates, a refrigerator, stacked boxes, and tall metal cabinets.

"Now where did I put it?" Becca says, rubbing her head. "I remember that day Zed came here so well…Mom calling out for me to help…Zed all filthy and scared. But when he looked into my eyes, there was this connection and…" Her voice catches.

"The fly mask," I remind her gently.

She bites her lip hard. "It should be here…but where?"

Leo closes the door behind us. "Becca, what do you remember about the last time you saw the fly mask?"

"It was stuck to Zed's face with blood and dirt, so I had to cut it off. Zed trusted me right away. He nuzzled my hand." She stops. "Anyway, when I washed the fly mask, I was surprised that it was trimmed in jewels. Not real, of course. Fake stones like dollar-store jewelry." Becca chuckles but it comes out more like a sob.

I squeeze her hand. "Then what happened to the mask?" I ask.

"Even filthy and torn, it looked expensive, so I asked Mom what to do with it."

"And she told you to…" Leo prompts.

"Put it in a box—over there." She points to a corner stacked with boxes.

"Let's start looking," Leo says cheerfully.

There are three shoe boxes, a midsize box, and two large ones. Becca can't remember the size of the box, so we each search a different box. I grab the smaller boxes, but one is full of napkins and the other is empty except for a bent horseshoe.

Leo groans when he opens the midsize box.

"What'd you find, Leo?" I ask, peering up from where I'm kneeling on the floor.

"Toilet paper. Rolls and rolls of it."

"Animal leashes and collars in this one," Becca says as she peers into the largest box. "Nothing for horses except this blue halter. No fly masks."

We search the rest of the room, from beneath the sink to cabinets and shelves.

"Eureka!" Leo shouts.

Becca and I spin around.

"Look what I found on the floor!" Leo holds out a tear-shaped blue stone the size of a quarter.

"I remember that jewel!" Becca jumps up excitedly. "It was the center stone in the fly mask. The other gems were smaller, purple and black."

"Even dirty it still shines," I marvel.

"Like a sapphire." Becca takes the jewel from Leo, cupping it in her palm. "What if it's a *real* sapphire?"

"No," Leo replies. "According to my calculations of its size, density, and coloring, this jewel is 100 percent fake. If you look closely, you can see where the blue color has flaked off. It isn't worth much."

"Except to Caleb's grandmother," I say.

Becca snaps her fingers. "I just remembered the box I put the fly mask in! It was large, cardboard, with red writing on the side."

"What did the writing say?" Leo asks.

"Something starting with a *D*. Or was it *B*?" Becca shakes her head. "None of these boxes look right. I'll have to ask Mom."

We find Becca's mom leaning against the horse trailer, talking to Caleb. She tosses back her dark curls and is laughing at something he said.

Caleb turns to Becca hopefully. "Did you find it?"

"No, but we found this." Becca holds up the blue stone.

Caleb's eyes light up as he reaches for the jewel. "It's from the mask!"

"Looks like a real sapphire," Becca says.

"Sure does." He holds up the stone so it catches the sunlight. "Nice shine for a fake."

Leo turns to Becca. "I told you it wasn't real."

"It's a real good imitation." Caleb pockets the stone, then looks questioningly at Becca. "So where's the fly mask?"

"I wish I knew." Becca holds out her arms in defeat.

"We searched the building," Leo adds. "But it wasn't there."

Becca's mother steps forward. "Did you search the cabinets?"

"Everywhere," Becca insists. "But I know I put it in a box. It was large, white, and in the corner by the sink. It had red writing, beginning with *D*."

"Oh no! Not that box!" Mrs. Morales gasps. "*D* is for donation."

"What do you mean?" Caleb asks, frowning.

"That box held items to donate to the Wear-Ever Thrift Store. But I dropped it off last month." Mrs. Morales wrings her hands. "The fly mask is gone."

- Chapter 6 -
A Plan

"I'm so sorry," Mrs. Morales says sadly. "I hope your grandmother isn't too disappointed."

"She won't be because I'm not leaving town without the mask," Caleb says with a determined press of his lips. "If it's still at that store, I'll find it. What's the address?"

"Corner of Main and Pleasant in downtown Sun Flower," she says.

I can't help but smile because locals call the three streets of businesses "downtown." Sun Flower is more a sprawling suburb with miles of houses than a "town." But people like to make the few businesses we have sound important.

Caleb clicks on his phone, and I read over his

shoulder. The tiny screen flashes *Wear-Ever Thrift* with a map, business hours, and a phone number.

When Caleb groans, I know he's noticed the business hours.

Weekdays: 8–4. Saturday: 9–4. Closed Sunday.

It's 5:14 p.m. on Saturday.

Caleb shoves the phone into his back pocket and mutters a word I'd get grounded for saying. "I reckon it'll have to wait," he says.

"The fly mask has probably been sold by now, but I'll check the store Monday morning," Mrs. Morales offers. "If I find it, I'll mail it to you."

"Mighty kind of you, but I'd best find it myself." Caleb pauses a moment, rubbing the stubble on his chin. "The mask means a lot to Grandma Ellie because it was the last gift Grandpa ever gave to her. I have a buddy who lives close by. I can bunk with him for a few nights." He looks into Mrs. Morales's face. "Would it be all right if the zorse stays until Monday?"

When Mrs. Morales says, "Of course, Zed can stay," Becca's face lights up in a smile bright enough to light every city in the world.

And I smile too.

A lot can happen in two days.

While the adults go into the house to talk, Becca turns to Leo and me with excited, dark eyes. "Meet me at the Skunk Shack," she whispers. "I'll join you there after I take Zed to the pasture."

"Aren't you staying with Zed?" I'm surprised because I thought Becca would spend every minute of her last days with Zed (probably even sneaking him into her room at night).

"I want to but we need to have an urgent CCSC meeting," she says. "Meet you at the shack soon."

I hop onto my bike and Leo clicks his remote to power up his gyro-board. The path up the hill is steep and I'm puffing hard by the time I reach the top. Leo, zooming on robotic wheels, isn't even sweating.

When we walk into the Skunk Shack, two kittens scamper toward us.

"Did you miss me, Honey?" I pick up my sweet, orange fur baby.

Leo's kitten now lives at his house, so he scoops up Becca's black-and-white kitty, Chris (named after her fashion idol Christian Dior). The kittens meow like they're hungry, although Becca fed them before Caleb Hunter arrived.

"What do you think Becca wants to talk about?" I ask Leo as I dangle a string. Honey swats it with her paw.

"I don't know," Leo says as he tickles Chris under the chin.

"She said it was urgent." A scary thought hits me. "Do you think she's planning to run away with Zed?"

"She's too smart for that," Leo says.

"But she's desperate to keep him. What if she asks us to help her hide Zed like we're doing with the kittens?"

"We can't hide a zorse in here," Leo says with a gesture around the small shack. "Zed is large, energetic, and noisy."

"That's for sure," I agree. "He'd end up kicking out walls and smashing the window. And if Becca's mom organized a search party, they'd look here and find not just Zed but our kittens too."

"That would be very bad." Leo glances down at the kitten in his arms.

"Our secret clubhouse wouldn't be secret anymore," I add, thinking how much I love being part of the CCSC and meeting in our clubhouse. I don't want it to ever end.

But it may end for me—if my family has to move away.

I still need to get ideas from my friends about finding a job for Dad. But that will have to wait till later.

Kneeling down on the wood floor, I wiggle the string for Honey to chase. Chris jumps out of Leo's arm to paw the string too. Leo goes over to the grandfather clock, metal pinging as he sorts through a pile of parts. I keep on playing with the kittens. They get distracted by a bug creeping up the wall. Honey pounces on the bug but misses. Chris jumps higher, but the bug crawls out of reach, and Chris somersaults to the floor, landing gracefully on his paws.

"They're so cute," I say, laughing as I gesture for Leo to watch the kittens.

"They'll never catch that bug. It's much too high and—" He stops, staring at me. "Why are you wearing Becca's necklace?"

I reach up to touch my Sparkler necklace. I had hoped Leo wouldn't notice. I've been hiding it underneath my shirt, so he doesn't feel left out. Drats.

"Um…it's mine," I say.

He leans closer to study the necklace. "Did Becca give it to you?"

"No. It's from the Sparklers. They all wear these necklaces." He looks even more confused so I blurt out, "Didn't you see me sitting with them at lunch?"

"No."

"I thought someone observant like you would have noticed."

"I'm observant when it matters. I shut out distractions during lunch to concentrate on calculations on my tablet. I'm working on a microsized drone that will be an efficient surveillance tool."

I might as well be talking to a drone. "The Sparklers invited me into their group temporarily, so I can help them plan a fund-raiser," I tell him. "And they gave me this sparkly necklace."

"The stones are artificial gems made of paste, glass, or gem quarts that are cut into facets to make them sparkle," he says while studying me like I'm a test subject for an experiment he can't figure out. I can almost see gears churning in his head. Are they processing anger, envy, or hurt?

Me, I'm processing guilt. If I found out Becca and Leo were in a group without me, I'd feel left out. I should have sat with Leo at lunch. I wanted to... but I wanted to sit with the Sparklers more. Now I have new friends, and Leo's more alone than ever.

"I'll only hang with the Sparklers for a few weeks, and Becca and I won't tell them anything about the CCSC," I assure him. "Becca and I will still meet here after school, take care of the kittens, and go biking to look for lost animals. So don't feel bad."

"Why would I?" He shrugs. "You're stuck with those glitter-brains. I feel sorry for you."

"*You're* sorry for *me*?" I glare at him.

"Yes." He turns his attention back to the broken clock.

Unbelievable! Leo so doesn't get it. I rub my fingers over the crescent-moon necklace. It's an honor to be an honorary Sparkler. The best part was when Becca told the other girls that I was interesting and smart. It'll be fun to be almost popular for a few weeks. And the best part will be sharing the Sparklers with Becca.

The crunch of footsteps outside jerks me to alertness. The door bursts open and frightened kittens scatter. Becca rushes into the room, out of breath like she ran all the way up the hill.

"Wait till you hear my plan!" she exclaims, flipping her ponytail over her shoulder.

Leo stands stiffly. "Is this an official CCSC meeting?"

"It can be if you want it to." Becca picks up her kitten and pulls out her chair at the table.

"Then we need to sit at the table and call the meeting to order," Leo says.

It's easier to go along with Leo than argue, so Becca and I sit with him at the table. We grab drinks from the cooler and some chips, then wait for Leo to talk.

"The CCSC meeting is called to order," he says with his chin held high and papers in his hand. "Is there any old business to discuss?"

"No," Becca says impatiently. "Skip ahead to the new business."

"Clubs run on rules," he goes on. "Following *Robert's Rules of Order* maintains fairness and democracy."

"Says the dictator," I whisper to Becca.

"I heard that but I choose to ignore it." Leo picks up his papers. "I'll begin with the treasurer's report."

Becca groans. "Can we skip that so I can tell you my plan?"

"With cat food, litter, and other expenses, our treasury has twenty-four dollars and twenty-seven cents," Leo goes on. "I can show you the exact figures and expenditures."

"Not now," I say. "I want to hear Becca."

Leo gives me a stern look. "Impatience is a waste of time."

"You're the one wasting time," I argue. "We can do boring club business later."

"Finances are not boring," he says. "They are fun."

"Only to you," I say, then turn to Becca. "So what's going on? Is this about Zed?"

"No, his fly mask." Becca pauses to eat a chip. "I've been on the phone with Sophia's cousin Devin."

"Who?" Leo asks.

"Sophia is from the Sparklers and her cousin Devin is the assistant manager for the Wear-Ever Thrift Store," Becca explains. "I've only met Devin a few times, but I'd heard he likes my friend Christin's older sister, Amanda. I promised to hook him up with Amanda, which is easy because she already likes him but is too shy to tell him."

"Huh?" Leo looks confused, but I totally get it. Becca is so genuine and friendly that people open up to her.

"I have a plan to help Zed." Becca pauses then adds sadly, "I know Zed has to leave and I'm glad the grandmother will be with him again. But she's old. What will happen when she's gone? I heard Caleb tell Mom he's joining the rodeo circuit, which means lots of traveling, and he'll ride a horse, not a zorse. How can Caleb take care of Zed when he's traveling?"

"Caleb mentioned a sister," Leo says. "She'll probably keep Zed."

"But what if she doesn't?" Becca waves her hands dramatically. "Zed deserves to be with the person who loves him best. And that would be me."

I hate to burst her happy bubble. Still....

"Becca, be realistic." I gently put my hand on hers. "Once Zed is gone, your mother won't let him come back. She won't even let you keep a small kitten."

"Only because I haven't told her about Chris," Becca argues, petting the ball of black-and-white fur curled on her lap. "If I ask her now, she'll say we have too many animals. So I'll ask after the humane society fund-raiser when most of our foster animals will be adopted. Mom won't have an excuse to say no to a cat or a zorse."

Leo shakes his head. "Caleb won't give you a valuable zorse for free."

"He might if he's grateful because I did something

huge for him," Becca says with a confident smile. "Then when his grandma can't take care of Zed anymore, Caleb will bring him back to me."

"And why would he do that?" Leo asks skeptically.

"Because I'm going to find the jeweled fly mask for him tonight." She grins at us. "And you're going to help me."

- Chapter 7 -
Sunflower Mary

I left the Skunk Shack hours ago, but I haven't been able to think of anything except Becca's fly mask plan.

I'm not sure whether to be excited or scared. I've longed to go on thrilling missions since I read my first James Bond novel. But I thought I'd have to wait until I was a grown-up or at least a teenager. Instead, tonight I'm searching a closed store.

I pull my spy pack down from its hiding spot in the back of the high closet shelf. It looks like an ordinary green backpack but is filled with cool stuff. It's heavy, so I'll carry only what I need. Last week was my first chance to use it on a for-real stakeout. It was exciting but not scary. But this time we're not just watching from the outside—we're going *inside*.

In spy novels, detectives break into buildings all the time like it's no big deal. If they get arrested, they're quickly released or escape. But I'd freak out if I got arrested. And my parents would ground me forever.

I'm glad we have permission to go into the building. Unfortunately, the assistant manager, Devin, can't meet us there since he has tickets to an opera in San Francisco. But he's leaving us a key.

"He was rushing out the door when I called," Becca explained. "He only had time to tell me the alarm code and where to find the key. Oh, and he couldn't get in touch with his boss, so he said to stay out of sight and don't turn on the lights."

I'll need a flashlight, I think as I dig into my spy pack for my flash cap. I made it myself by attaching a light on a sports cap. The light may be tiny, but the beam is powerful.

Should I bring my black knit cap? I ponder. It covers my face and has eyeholes like a mask. But it's itchy and cuts off my peripheral vision. Since we have permission to go into the store, why hide my identity? So that would be a no.

What about my lock picks? I jingle the ring of different shaped picks in my hand. They don't weigh much, but why take them when we'll have a key? The assistant store manager told Becca he hid the key beneath a decorative stone turtle by the back door. Once we have the key, we will disable the alarm, unlock the door, find the fly mask, reset the alarm, and return the key.

Our mission is more like shopping than spying.

So why do I have a bad feeling?

"Don't be silly," I tell myself, then get back to work.

I sort through my spy pack, taking out things I won't need, like the small mirror, laser pointer, bottle of graphite powder, plastic rain jacket, and energy bars.

What I leave in the spy pack:

Magnifying glass

Plastic gloves (never a good idea to leave fingerprints)

Roll of wire

Plastic baggies

Mini tool kit

Duct tape (I read a book called *101 Uses for Duct Tape*)

Flash cap

I'll use the baggies to wrap up two BLT sandwiches, so when I tell Mom I'm eating dinner with Becca, it won't be a lie. I just won't tell her *where* we're eating dinner.

My spy pack feels light on my back as I hop on my bike and pedal for Pleasant Street. It's only a few miles to Wear-Ever Thrift. The store is at the east end of downtown and backs up into a park with shady trees that will give us cover until we're covertly inside the store.

As a precaution, I stay off busy streets and wind through random side streets.

I'm not sure how it happens, but suddenly I'm at the edge of downtown, where the houses are older than the paved streets. Driveways are so narrow, cars spill over to the sidewalk or are parked on front yards like lawn ornaments.

From what I can see over fence tops, most yards are too small for a large dog to play fetch in. Thinking of dogs makes me miss Handsome. He loves to chase his Frisbee. I call him a "golden whip" because he's part golden retriever and part whippet—two very energetic breeds blended into the best dog ever. Even though he's huge, he used to curl up every night on my bed. When we lost our house, he moved in with Gran Nola. Now I only see him when I visit my grandmother.

I'm a block away from Pleasant Street when I slow down for yellow — not a traffic yield sign, but a fairy-tale cottage with a front yard glorious with sunflowers. There must be hundreds of stalks of golden flowers taller than me.

It's the most gorgeous garden ever! I stop my bike, balancing on my tiptoes, and admire the flowers. They're like a crowd of smiling faces, as if each sunflower represents a resident of Sun Flower and they're gathered together to party.

"Well, don't just gawk, missy. Come on over," a crackly voice calls.

I look around but can't see through the blooming yard. I roll my bike a few feet until I see the tiny, wrinkled woman stepping off the porch. Her face is crinkled with age, but her black eyes shine bright. And she's hobbling surprisingly fast on her cane. She wears a flowing, mustard-yellow skirt with a white blouse trimmed in tiny brown beads.

"Don't be shy," she says sweetly, her amber, tear-shaped earrings dangling as she leans against her cane. The cane's wooden handle is a carved sunflower. "Come visit with me. It isn't often young folks stop by, and I get lonely."

"Um...I can't stay. I'm meeting friends."

"There's always time to find for a chat with Sunflower Mary. Everyone around here knows me and I know more about them than some would like," she adds with a chuckle. "You're the baker's daughter, aren't you?"

"You know Dad?" I ask, surprised.

"Never forgot the taste of his hot cinnamon croissants. Shame the café closed down. But a skilled baker will quickly find a new job."

Not so *quickly*, I think.

"Come closer, dear." She holds out a gnarled hand, her misshapen fingers glittering with rings.

"I really should go," I say, my foot poised for a quick pedal kick off.

"Weave the stars with the sun, and this is what you get." She holds out her clasped hand. "I made it myself."

Now I'm too curious to leave. She seems harmless and even knows my dad.

I prop up my bike on the kickstand and take a cautious step toward her. She unfolds her fingers and in the palm of her hand is a yarn flower, golden bright enough to make the sun jealous. At the center of the flower, tiny beads shimmer.

No—not beads.

Sunflower seeds.

"Beautiful," I say with awe, caressing the soft yarn.

"A gift for you," she says in a raspy voice. "Turn it over, dear. See the clasp? Pin it on your shirt. It'll never wither like a real sunflower."

It's pretty, like an accessory the Sparklers would wear. But I shake my head. "I can't take it."

"My yarn flowers are made to be shared. Some people say they don't know what came first—Sun Flower the town or Sunflower Mary. At one time or another, almost everyone in Sun Flower wore one of my yarn flowers. We're all one big family here, you know. Some of us just haven't met yet. Pin your flower right over your heart."

She's staring up at me with such eagerness that I can't refuse. I fiddle with the clasp until I fasten it to my shirt.

"Beautiful!" She claps her wrinkled hands. "Wear it proudly."

"I will," I promise, touched that someone I just met would give me a gift. "I wish I had something for you."

She points to my neck. "Sure would love a shiny necklace like that," she says with a sly smile.

I touch my crescent necklace. "Oh…I can't give this away."

"I would never ask you to do that. I'm sure it means a lot to you. Such a pretty necklace must have a special meaning."

"It does," I say. "A friend gave it to me."

Her silvery brows rise to points. "A handsome young man?"

"No!" I blush. "It's a club thing. A bunch of us girls wear them."

"Oh, a club insignia. I do so enjoy clubs…especially secret ones," she says. "Is your club secret?"

Not this one, I think with a shake my head. "Everyone at school knows about the Sparklers."

"I love things that sparkle," she adds like she's confiding in me, but her gaze is on my necklace. "You take good care of that necklace and your yarn flower too. If anyone asks, tell them Sunflower Mary gave it to you."

"I will. Thank you," I say, then push off on my bike.

As I wheel away, I'm not sure what to think of the old woman. Her garden is beautiful, and it was kind of her to give me a gift. But the way she stared at my necklace was creepy—like she wanted to rip it off my neck.

And I get a strange feeling of being watched.

I glance back over my shoulder.

But all I see is Sunflower Mary's back as she disappears into her house.

- Chapter 8 -
Shadows

Seconds later, I roll my bike up to the back of the Wear-Ever Thrift Store.

The sun is setting, but it won't be dark for another hour. Still the store looks like it's already gone to sleep: lights shut off, blinds closed, and an empty parking lot.

I park my bike so it's hidden beneath a shady tree, then walk around to the back door where I find my friends. Leo's shoulders are hunched as he fiddles with an alarm panel next to the door. I walk over to Becca. She's kneeling on the ground, dressed all in black from her laced leather boots to her stretchy, long-sleeved shirt; her long ponytail is the exception, as it's tied in leopard-print bows.

"What are you doing?" I ask, peering over her shoulder at a stone turtle as big as my backpack.

"Getting the key." She grabs the brownish green turtle shell with both hands. "It should be under here."

"Do you need help lifting it?"

"No, it's hollow so it's not very heavy." She reaches beneath the stone turtle, then holds out a small brassy key. "Found it!"

"Yay you," I say, clapping.

Standing, Becca wipes her hands off on her black jeans; then, she points to my shirt. "You got sunflowered."

"Sunflowered?" I run my fingers over the soft yarn. "Is that a real word?"

"Around here it is," Becca says with a chuckle.

"You know Sunflower Mary?"

"Sure. Who doesn't?"

"Me, I guess," I admit. "My old neighborhood was too far from downtown, so I wasn't allowed to bike there."

"Even I know who Sunflower Mary is," Leo adds as he turns toward us. "The alarm is disabled. All I need is the key to the door, and we're in."

"Here." Becca tosses the key, and Leo catches it

with one hand. "Anyway, Sunflower Mary is like our town mascot. Before she hurt her hip, almost every day, she'd sit outside the post office and pass out yarn sunflowers."

"Like this one," I say with a nod toward my shirt. "Now that you mention it, I do remember hearing about a crazy flower lady."

"She's not crazy. She's nice," Becca says, sitting down on the stone turtle. "She gave me my first yarn flower when I was six. I wore it for weeks until I forgot to take it off and tossed my shirt in the laundry basket. All that was left was tangled yellow yarn. But the next day, I found a new yarn flower in a box on my porch."

"How did she know your flower was ruined?" I ask.

"Mom probably told her."

"Yeah, that makes sense," I say, but I get a prickly feeling and remember the strange way Sunflower Mary stared at me—like she could read minds.

"Becca," Leo calls out in a sharp tone. "You gave me the wrong key."

"Did not," Becca says.

"The key doesn't fit," he insists.

"Of course it does." Becca goes over to Leo.

"Notice the grooves and size." Leo holds up the

key to show her. "It doesn't match the door lock."

"But it has to be the right key," Becca argues. "Devin told me it would be under the turtle."

"Yeah," I agree. "I saw Becca take it from the turtle."

Leo purses his lips. "Then why doesn't it fit the lock?"

"Maybe you're doing it wrong," I say. "Did you turn it upside down?"

"The direction does not change the fact that it's the incorrect size," he says with an insulted sniff.

"Let me try." I take the key from his hand, poke, jiggle, and shove, but it still doesn't fit.

Leo folds his arms over his chest and gives me an "I told you so" look.

Becca shakes her head. "I found it exactly where Devin said to look, and there's only one turtle statue."

"He must have left the wrong key," I say.

"Obviously, but that won't be a problem." She gives me an eager look. "You can open the door, Kelsey, with your lock picks."

"Uh...about my picks..." I hang my head. "I don't have them."

"Aren't they in there?" Becca says, pointing.

"They *were*." I groan. "But my spy pack gets so heavy, I only brought what I thought I'd need. And you told me we had a key."

"The wrong key." Becca twists her ponytail around her fingers. "Now what are we going to do?"

"I might be able to open the lock with a twisted wire," I say.

Leo steps forward. "Or we can use my key spider."

"A spider can't open a lock," I argue.

"Yeah," Becca says. "Although spiders are cool. We had a Chilean rose tarantula at the sanctuary for a while. He was soft and gentle."

"Not a fan of spiders." I watch Leo as he reaches into his pocket.

When he holds out his hand, I jump back until I realize he's not holding a creepy spider. His "key spider" looks like a clump of keys melted together with metal twisted out like spider legs.

"I got the idea from your lock picks, Kelsey. Rotating gears spin into different key shapes." Leo spins a dial on the metal sphere. "Multiple keys in a compact device flat enough to fit inside a pocket. See? I just spin the dial until I get the right key shape. Like this," he says as he aims for the lock.

Click. The door swings open.

"You did it, Leo!" Becca pats him on the shoulder.

"Great tool," I say a bit enviously because it works better than my lock picks.

Leo holds it out to me. "Would you like my key spider?"

"But it's yours. I can't take it."

"It's only the first model. The next one will be improved, and I'll keep that one so I'm ready the next time I get handcuffed."

"Thanks." I bounce the key spider in my hand, pleased that Leo would give me one of his inventions. "A spy can never have too many lock picks."

Becca opens the door. "I've shopped here a lot, so I'll lead." She aims her flashlight to shine a path across crowded aisles. It's still light outside but dark as a tomb in the store.

"Anyone need a flashlight?" Becca asks. "I brought an extra."

"I've got a flash cap." I point to my sports cap, switching on the light above the brim. "I taped on a light, and it works almost as good as the ones in my spy catalogs."

"I like it." Leo approves, then pulls out a pair of goggles from his shirt pocket. "I brought these to see better in the dark. They're infrared with night vision."

We all aim our lights forward and enter the store.

"Let's split up to search for the box," I suggest.

"Yeah," Becca agrees. "But the fly mask won't be in a box anymore. It will be on display. I'll look in clothing racks."

"The jewelry table is the logical place to search," Leo says.

I choose the pet aisle.

My cap's beam is narrow, so I swivel my head back and forth as I go through aisles, to the left side of the store, where I find a table full of pet accessories—leashes, chew toys, cat climbers, pet carriers, and everything you can imagine for animals. Lots of cute stuff I'd love to buy for Honey. But this isn't about shopping—it's a search-and-recover mission.

I dig through shelves of horse accessories: blankets, halters, ropes, curry combs, and even a box of old horseshoes. I find a fly mask, only it's plain black netting with fringe trim instead of jewels.

"Drats," I mutter.

I peer around dim shapes of shelves and displays and wonder where to search next. What if the mask was mistaken for a different kind of mask?

Excited by this idea, I head over to the costume corner. I came here last Halloween for a costume and found a wicked monster mask. It was shockingly gross, with scarred skin, a ripped ear, and a bloody hole for a nose. I find a zombie mask that's even more disgusting on a table heaped with creepy, cute, and every kind of mask imaginable—except a fly mask.

Discouraged, I slump over to Becca in the clothes area. A fly mask doesn't belong with clothes, but it could be mistaken for a scarf or hair net. We check boxes, shelves, and hanging racks.

But no mask.

When we join Leo, it's the same thing. So we regroup by the cash register, keeping our lights low, so they can't be seen through windows.

"According to my calculations," Leo says wearily, "it will take an hour and thirty-six minutes to search the entire store."

"I can't stay that long," I say. "I have to be home by six."

"My curfew is before dark." Becca glances through the storefront window. "Mom doesn't want me riding my bike at night."

"I need to go home too, to feed my kitten," Leo adds.

I frown. "I hate giving up, but I think someone bought the fly mask."

"Which means I have no way of impressing Caleb Hunter," Becca says. "Zed will leave and I'll never see him again."

"Ask Caleb if you can visit," I say, trying to cheer her up. "Nevada isn't that far away."

"As if my mother will drive me." Becca scowls. "Thanks for trying to help, but coming here was a waste of time. We might as well leave."

Keeping my flash cap low, I follow Becca through aisles, toward the back of the store. We're almost to the back door when there's a thud from outside.

"Did you hear that?" I whisper.

"What?" Becca asks.

"A thud like...like *that*!" I know by Becca's jump and Leo's gasp that they've heard it too.

"Footsteps!" Leo exclaims, pointing to the storefront window.

We swivel toward the large storefront window. Our lights join together to illuminate the darkened glass, reflecting back to us—but not before a shadowy figure shifts across the window.

Someone is out there.

- Chapter 9 -
Monster Mash

"If we can see him, he can see us!" I warn. "Duck down!"

"Turn off your lights!" Becca adds as we all drop to the floor.

It's so dark I can barely see my friends crouched beside me. And when I blink in blackness, ordinary shapes seem sinister: a clothes rack towers like a ferocious dragon and a store mannequin grabs for me with skeletal claws.

"Is he still out there?" Becca whispers beside me.

I lift my head toward the front window but can't see anything except the glow from a streetlight. Leo's goggles have night vision, so I ask, "Can you see anyone out the window?"

"No one is there," he answers.

"But that doesn't mean he's gone," I say uneasily.

"He?" Becca questions. "So you think it's a man?"

"Not sure. I could only make out a shadowy figure distorted against the window—no face, only darkness."

"It might have been a security guard," Leo suggests.

"Devin would have told me if there were a guard," Becca says.

"I'll go out the back and look around." Leo starts to rise, but I pull him down.

"Don't!" I say. "The shadow dude could be armed and dangerous."

"I'm not afraid," Leo assures, straining his neck to see over the table we're hiding behind. "I think he's gone anyway."

"Unless he went around the back," Becca says ominously. "Leo, you were the last inside. Did you lock the door?"

"I was more interested in unlocking it. I'll check to make sure it's locked," Leo says, rising.

"Be careful," Becca warns.

"I'm always careful." He hurries down the aisle.

"I don't think it's a security guard out there," I

whisper to Becca. "A guard would have a flashlight and keys. It might be a thief."

Light illuminates Becca's face when she clicks on her phone. "I'm calling 911."

"And tell them someone is trying to break into a store we already broke into? They'll call the manager, who doesn't know that his assistant manager left us a key."

"A key that didn't fit," Becca adds.

"Which makes us look like thieves," I say.

Becca groans. "What's taking Leo so long anyway?"

I'm wondering the same thing. I hope he hasn't done anything dumb, like confront the shadow dude. Leo's so logical that he forgets to be afraid. I kind of admire that.

Beside me, I feel Becca trembling. It's weird how stress has reversed our personalities. Usually Becca is the confident, nurturing one, but now I'm comforting her. And Leo has gone all superhero instead of nerdy sidekick.

"I really hate the dark," Becca says as she moves closer to me. "Let's talk, so I forget to be afraid. Want to hear a secret? Something not even the Sparklers know?"

Secret—my favorite word. "Tell me."

"Okay. But if the other Sparklers knew, they'd tease me. You can't tell anyone."

"I would never do that," I promise.

Becca sucks in a deep breath. "I can't go to sleep at night without a light."

"That's not embarrassing. Lots of people use a night-light."

"Do you?" she asks in an eager voice, like she hopes I'll say yes.

I love being in the dark (except when a scary shadow dude is outside). Darkness is like an invisible cloak that makes me feel brave and bold. When the lights go out, my other senses heighten; voices come in clearer, smells sharpen, and touch can lead to interesting discoveries.

Becca is waiting for my answer. I know she's nervous, so I say, "I have a night-light," which is true. My night-light is in the bottom of my dresser, still in the box my Aunt Louise gave me for my birthday. I never used it.

"What does it look like?"

"Um...just a light bulb."

"Mine is supercute. It's shaped like a dog with a wagging tail that changes colors. The light shines across my walls like a rainbow and...What's that noise?" Becca suddenly grips my arm. "Did you hear it?"

"What?" I touch my ear, listening.

"A scratchy sound," Becca says.

I lift my head toward the front of the store. Reflections and shadows waver, and I imagine someone bursting into the store so fast Becca doesn't have time to call 911.

My heart pounds, my courage stampeding away. I can't stop staring at the window, although there's no one there now. But he may still be out there— and we're trapped in here.

We huddle in an aisle between clothing racks. When I shift to get more comfortable, my elbow bumps into something soft. I look up at a distorted face with bloodshot eyes and fangs. I'm ready to scream until I realize it's just a Halloween mask on a mannequin. The mask is spongy latex, so it really looks eerily real—like a twisted human face. The hanging eye even blinks.

Who knew a thrift store could be so creepy?

"I'm freaking out," Becca confides. "Talk about something not scary."

"Like what?"

"School, kittens, or the Sparklers—we still need a fund-raiser idea."

"You said something *not* scary," I tease, and when she laughs, her ponytail tickles across my arm. The yellow part of her leopard-print ponytail tie shimmers in the dark—which gives me an idea.

"We could sell animal-print hair ties," I suggest.

"Except the other girls can't sew." She looks at me hopefully. "Can you?"

"No. But you could teach me."

"It'll be quicker to sew them myself." She sighs. "Chloe has all these big ideas—volunteering to collect canned goods, candy sale fund-raisers, and now we're manning a booth—but guess who ends up doing the work?"

I point to her.

"Tragically true," she says wearily. "I had already volunteered to help out with the Humane Society Fund-raiser but now I have double the responsibilities. Chloe is too busy bossing everyone around to do actual work. Sophia has drama club practice. And Tyla puts things off until it's too late. I love the girls, but they make me crazy. That's why I almost—" Becca breaks off, then leans close to whisper in my ear. "I was going to quit the Sparklers."

"Wow," I say, shocked.

"I was tired of being bossed around. I get that enough at home. But when I told Chloe, she begged me to stay. I said I would on one condition."

"What?"

I can barely make out her hand pointing toward me. "That you join the Sparklers. All but one person wanted you to join, so we compromised on your becoming a temporary member and helping with the fund-raiser."

"Let me guess," I say. "Tyla voted against me."

"Don't take it personally. She is just naturally disagreeable. But I got my way. And I made sure you had a silver necklace too."

Even though I'm trapped inside a store with a scary dude outside, I smile.

Since Becca confided in me, I want to share with her. So I tell her about losing our home, moving to the apartment, and Dad's disappointing job search.

"You must miss your house so much," she says sympathetically.

"I miss Handsome more," I tell her. "But the worse part is that if Dad can't find a job soon, we'll have to leave Sun Flower."

"No!" She clutches my hand. "I can't lose both Zed and you."

"It may not happen—it all depends on Dad finding a job." I hesitate. "But he needs help, so I thought we could make finding him a job a CCSC project."

"I'd love to help. I'll ask around about jobs," she offers. "My friends have friends, who have friends, who have friends—someone is sure to know of a job."

"Thanks!" I hug her. "And I'll tell Leo—"

"Tell Leo what?" Leo asks as he crouches beside us.

"You're safe!" I exclaim, relieved. "What took you so long?"

"After I locked the back door, I looked out the window but didn't see anyone. I also made sure the front door was locked." He tilts his head. "What did you want to tell me?"

Keeping my voice low, I say, "Well, my dad has been out of work, and I thought maybe the CCSC could help him find a job."

"I can look online," Leo offers. "I'll limit the search to local—"

"What was that?" I interrupt and jump at a metallic sound.

"It came from the back of the store!" Becca cries softly.

Leo pushes up his night vision goggles and looks

around. "Someone's jiggling the doorknob. It's locked, but that won't keep him out long."

"That's it! I'm calling 911." Light flashes from Becca's hand as she clicks on her phone. "I don't care if we get in trouble—we'll be safer in jail."

"They put kids in juvenile hall, not jail," Leo says.

"Safer there than in here with a monster outside," Becca says.

Her words trigger an idea.

"Don't call yet, Becca." I put my hand over her phone. "I'll be right back."

Before she can argue, I hurry away.

It's tempting to turn on my light, but I resist and feel my way down the aisle and over to a familiar table. I sort through a pile until I find what I'm looking for, then feel my way back.

The back door rattles again, with more force.

I scoot down between Becca and Leo. "Take these," I say, then I explain my idea.

Once we're ready, we stay close to each other as we feel our way down aisles, until we near the back door.

The rattling has stopped, replaced with a pinging metallic sound.

"He's picking the lock!" Leo whispers.

"Hurry," I say, slipping the latex mask over my face. "Let's do this."

"Mine's on," Becca answers in a muffled voice.

Leo drops his goggles, and they clunk on the ground. Then he slips on the mask I choose for him. "I'm ready," he tells me.

"Count of three, we go together," I say in a hushed voice, hoping this works. Because if it doesn't, the intruder will know we're here.

"One...two..." I fit the mask over my face. "Three!"

We jump to our feet then rush to the back door's window.

I'm wearing a zombie mask, Becca is a werewolf, and Leo is a vampire.

We squash our monster faces against the glass.

Outside, someone shrieks.

- Chapter 10 -
Clue in Blue

The shriek echoes like an unearthly creature and is completely unidentifiable as man, woman, or kid. I rush to the window and peer through my mask at a shadowy figure hurrying away. The figure falls, staggers up from the ground, then limps off.

I want to rush after him like the investigators in my spy books. They'd pursue the villain until they took him down, snapped on handcuffs, and hauled him off to jail. But the intruder is probably an adult (maybe carrying a gun or knife), and we're just kids.

We stay safely inside the store.

"He's gone." I rip off my itchy mask and turn my flash cap back on, so I can see my friends. "We scared him good."

"We sure did." Becca looks terrifying and hairy in her werewolf mask. "He was so scared, I bet he wet his pants."

"The masks were a great idea, Kelsey." Leo holds his vampire mask out by two fingers. "I'm coming back when the store is open to buy this one for Halloween. I'll have to practice saying, 'I vant to suck your blood.'"

"Zombies prefer brains for lunch." I jiggle my mask, so the hanging eyeball bobs like a yo-yo.

Becca takes off her mask. "It's soft like puppy fur," she says, running her fingers over the werewolf face like he's a cute pet she wants to take home.

Leo presses his hands against the window to peer out. "I wanted to follow him, but according to my calculations, the risks outweighed the results. Did you notice he was limping?"

"He tripped and fell," I say, giving the rubbery eyeball a flick with my finger to keep it wobbling. "Either of you get a good look at him?"

"When I looked for a face—" Becca sucks in a sharp breath. "There was nothing."

"He wore a hooded cape or jacket," Leo guesses. "He probably planned to rob the store."

"Why steal secondhand clothes and junk?" Becca asks skeptically.

"There might be money in the cash register," Leo replies.

"I'm glad he couldn't get in." I gather the monster masks. "He's gone now and should we go too."

After I return the masks to the costume table, we leave through the back door. The sun has slipped behind the trees, and the chilly air makes me shiver. I don't need to check my watch to know I'm late. I'll have to pedal fast to avoid the wrath of Dad.

But a thought occurs to me, and I point to the doorknob. "The intruder rattled the knob hard. I could dust for fingerprints."

"Only if you want to get mine," Leo says.

"Mine too," Becca says, holding up her hands and wiggling her fingers. "There must be hundreds of prints on the door."

"And the intruder may have been wearing gloves," Leo adds.

"Drats," I say with a sigh.

I'm disappointed about my lack of clues—until I spot something blue on the stone turtle's shell.

"Look!" I point excitedly. "The intruder dropped a pen."

"It could belong to anyone and have been there for weeks," Leo says.

Becca shakes her head. "It wasn't there when I lifted the turtle to get the key."

"He must have dropped the pen when he tripped over the turtle," I say, excitedly digging into my spy pack for my plastic gloves and a baggie. I slip on the gloves, then carefully pick up the pen and shine my cap light onto it. "See! This is a good clue. There's writing on the side."

"What?" Becca asks, peering over my shoulder.

"I think it's a business logo." I squint at the tiny writing. "Desert Sun Train…and another word that's faded."

"Desert Sun Train what?" Leo puzzles, rubbing his chin.

"I can't tell," I say, turning to Becca. "A train store?"

"We don't even have a toy store in Sun Flower."

"I think it came from far away, somewhere where there's a desert." I study the pen in the bright shine of my cap light. The faded word is short, only two or three letters.

"It could be from anywhere." Becca slumps her shoulders. "But it doesn't matter. The intruder has nothing to do with the fly mask. He probably didn't even know we were inside the store. I wish we could have found the fly mask."

"It might still be in the store," I say. "We could come back tomorrow."

Becca shakes her head. "That's my last full day with Zed. I'm staying with him."

"Leo," I turn to him. "Want to search again in the morning?"

"Negatory. My parents worked out a schedule so I spend Sundays with Dad. I don't know where we're going, but it'll be good to see Dad again," he says wistfully.

"There's nothing we can do here anyway. The mask is gone," Becca says. "Someone probably bought it weeks ago."

She's right, but I hate giving up—especially when I have a cool clue.

I carefully seal the blue pen in a protective baggie and label it "Evidence A." Not that it matters. Finding the intruder's identity won't help us find the fly mask.

Coming here was a complete waste of time.

Fly mask mission: fail.

Sunday morning, I check my email and there's an

attachment from Leo with a list of local jobs for my father: a hotel concierge, postal clerk, pest exterminator, animal control officer, and mortician's assistant.

I can't wait to tell Dad about these cool jobs, so I run downstairs and find him mixing batter for berry-spice crepes. But when I show him the list, he isn't impressed. "Pest control? A mortician's assistant?" He shakes his head. "I work with food. Not bugs or animals or dead people."

"But you need a job," I point out.

"Thanks but no thanks, Kels." He kisses my forehead, his eyes sad.

"At least keep the list and think about it."

"All right." The paper waves in his hand as he sets it aside on the counter. "But I'll find a job on my own."

Will it be in Sun Flower? I want to ask, but if I do, then he'll know I overheard his conversation with Mom.

Dad goes back to cooking our traditional Sunday brunch, ignoring the paper. He'll probably toss it in the trash once I leave.

This did not *go well*, I think as I slump to my room. But I'm not giving up until I find the right job for Dad.

In the meantime, I have a clue to figure out.

I shut my bedroom door and lock it because my sisters have a habit of bursting in without knocking. I set my spy pack on my bed, then unzip a narrow side pocket and take out the baggie with my blue clue.

It's important to always bag evidence. I slip on plastic gloves, then carefully take out the blue pen and place it on my desk. My fingerprinting kit and magnifying glass are ready.

The pen looks ordinary and inexpensive. It could be just a random pen, no importance at all. Or it could be the clue that leads to the intruder's identity.

I shine my desk lamp on the pen to study it. It's six inches long, with a dark-blue cap that's been chewed on. I deduce the ink is black by scribbling the word "clue" on a piece of paper. The printed logo runs from the bottom to the cap: Desert Sun Train...and a faded third word.

Lifting my magnifying glass, I try to make out the tiny writing. The first letter looks like it might be an *l*, *b*, or *d*. The second letter looks round and is most likely a vowel. I have no idea whether there's another letter or it's just a smudge.

For more info, I'll need the computer. But when I go into the living room, my sisters are already there, their dark-brown heads bent close as they giggle over photos—all photos of shirtless guys with six-pack abs.

When my sisters finally get off the computer, Dad announces breakfast is ready. The crepes are delicious.

When I finally sit at the computer, I run a local search for "Desert Sun Train."

No train businesses, not even a train station. And nothing called "Desert Sun." And why would there be? Sun Flower isn't near the desert. So I spread out my search to southern California, and the results include a newspaper and nudist colony in Palm Springs (hundreds of miles south). The closest hit I find for Desert Sun is a tanning salon thirty miles away. The faded word in the pen could be "tan" but that has nothing to do with a train. Still, it can't hurt to check it out. I try the phone number but get a recording saying they're closed on Sundays. (Why can't the rest of the world realize that detectives work seven days a week?)

Frustrated enough to throw the computer out the window, I power it down and grab a Frisbee.

A short bike ride later, I roll up to my grandmother's door.

"I was hoping you'd visit," Gran Nola says as she invites me in. She's wearing purple tights and a black exercise suit, and her hair is pulled back in a knot. She teaches yoga but not usually on the weekends.

"Did I interrupt anything?" I ask, glancing around but not seeing anyone else.

"No, just working on my Shooting Bow and Dolphin Plank pose. But I'm ready for a break. I've missed you this week—and so has Handsome."

"Sorry, I meant to come, but I've been busy."

"With your new friends?" she asks, opening the fridge and offering me a chilled berry drink.

"Yeah," I answer.

"Tell me about them," she says, leading me into the living room, where we take our usual seats (recliner for her and couch for me).

Gran Nola is so cool. I can tell her anything—except secrets. So I tell her about Becca being sad because Zed is leaving and how Leo is so smart, he designs robots, but I don't mention the kittens, clubhouse, or CCSC.

"Poor Becca," Gran Nola says. "It's always hard to let go of a pet."

I nod. "At least when I had to give up Handsome, he didn't move far away."

"And you can visit him whenever you want," Gran Nola says warmly. "Keeping Handsome is a win-win for me because he's great company and I get to see you more often."

"I don't come just to see Handsome," I assure her.

"I know." She hugs me, then hands me the Frisbee I set on the coffee table. "But I know you're eager to see him, and he could use some exercise."

Playing with Handsome is always fun. I love the echoing sound of his bark and how his big tongue tickles when he licks me. After we play with the Frisbee, I take him for a walk. He tugs and pulls, so it's exhausting keeping up with him.

As we go up and down sidewalks, I keep my eyes open for lost pets.

You'd be surprised how many animals run off or get lost. Some are stolen too, which is the worst. Becca, Leo, and I recently solved a pet-napping mystery, which reunited lots of animals with their owners. Although we did it to help people, some owners insisted on giving us rewards. Most of the money went to buy food and supplies for our kittens, some was donated to the Humane Society, and the rest went into the CCSC treasury.

I always carry a list of lost animals. There are currently only three missing pets listed: Milo, a Manx cat; an African parrot; and an elderly dachshund named Ditzy.

When I near Sunny Slope Park, I see a cocker spaniel without a collar chasing after a squirrel. The squirrel scampers up an oak, and the dog barks at the tree. The dog's apricot coat shines like he's been brushed recently. I'm just about to go over to him when a woman runs up to the dog, holding a leash with a dangling collar.

"False alarm," I murmur as the woman hugs the runaway dog, then fastens the collar around his neck.

Handsome jerks on my leash, so I jog to keep up with him.

When I get back to my grandmother's house, she holds out her phone to me. "For you, Kelsey," she says.

"Mom or Dad?" I guess since they like to check up on me.

"Neither." Gram takes the dog leash from me. "I'll put Handsome in the backyard while you talk to your friend."

Curious, I hold the phone to my ear.

"Kelsey!" Becca exclaims. "Wait till you hear!"

"Hear what?" I learn forward on the edge of the couch. "And how did you know to call me here?"

"Your mom gave me the number. I couldn't wait to tell you—Devin called me."

"Devin?" My memory clicks. "The assistant store manager."

"Exactly. He apologized for mixing up the keys and offered to let us into the store today, except I said we couldn't."

I grip the phone. "I hope you didn't tell him we picked the lock."

"No way. He thinks we couldn't get inside. But I felt I should warn him about the intruder, so I told him we scared off someone trying to break into the store."

"What did he say?"

"That it was probably a homeless person looking for a place to sleep. He felt so bad for leaving the wrong key that he said he'd bend store rules and check the computer for the fly mask. And guess what he found?"

"What?" I ask eagerly.

"The mask was sold to someone at our school."

Becca's voice rises with excitement. "The drama club has the fly mask."

Chapter 11

Staged

Monday morning, my alarm shocks me out of a great dream in which I'm moving into a country home with acres of fields for Handsome to run, a climbing tree for Honey, and a rope swing for me.

I slam off the alarm buzzer, then yawn and stumble out of bed. Way too early for school but Becca, Leo, and I are meeting with a seventh grader named Frankie. Becca found out from Sophia that Frankie is in charge of the drama club costumes, and he's usually backstage in the auditorium before school.

As I reach for a plain blue T-shirt from my closet, I think enviously of Becca's chic outfits. I don't have animal-print clothes, but my twin sisters received matching leopard-print shirts for their birthday. These cute shirts hang abandoned in their closet because my sisters won't wear lookalike clothes. I could ask for one of the shirts, but they only pass down old clothes to me.

They won't mind my borrowing a shirt— especially if I don't tell them.

I creep out of my room and to their door. I hear steady breathing, so I know they're still sleeping. Quietly, I open the door and peek inside. Kiana is hidden in her tangled blankets while Kenya has kicked off her blankets and has one foot poking over the edge of her bed.

Holding my breath, I walk on tiptoes, a trick I learned from *How to Be a Spy 101*. I step over discarded clothes and shoes. Their closet is on Kenya's side of the room. I'm halfway there when Kenya makes a wheezing noise like a sneeze. Startled, I trip over a discarded shoe but catch myself by grabbing onto Kenya's desk. Quick as a breath, I duck into the closet, shut the door behind me, and click a mini flashlight.

So many clothes! Most are on hangers but some are tossed on the floor. My sisters are such slobs. Still it doesn't take long to find the leopard-print shirts. They're identical except one looks smaller, so I grab it.

Snapping off the light, I slip out of the closet and tiptoe out of their room and back to mine. Success! Not only is the shirt cute, but it has pockets. And guess what I find in one of the pockets? A parking receipt for an over-eighteen club where my under-eighteen sisters aren't allowed. My sisters would be in *big* trouble if my parents saw this receipt.

Luckily for them, I can keep a secret.

The leopard shirt is too big, but a black belt solves that problem, and it looks great over my best pair of black jeans. For the final sparkly touch, I fasten on my crescent-moon necklace.

After a speedy bike ride to school, I find Becca waiting at my locker. She's wearing a zebra-print skirt with a clingy black top and black teardrop earrings.

"Where's Leo?" I ask, as I unlock my lock and put in my sack lunch, which smells sugary-sweet from Dad's cookies.

"He texted to say he would be seven minutes late."

"That's so Leo," I say with a laugh. "Even when he's late, he's precise."

I glance up, expecting Becca to laugh too. But she's pale, and her eyes are red, like she's been crying. "What's wrong, Becca?" I ask. "Has Zed left already?"

"Not yet." She sniffs. "But he'll be gone by tonight."

"I'm so sorry." I wrap her in a hug. "He's going to be okay—and so are you. You should be used to animals leaving. You live on a sanctuary where animals find new homes all the time."

"I know…" Her voice catches and she wipes her eyes. "It's just that Zed is special. We got really close, and he even lets me ride him. I'm going to miss him so much."

"I wish I could help."

"Talking about it helps a little. I know you love animals too and understand how it feels when one leaves."

I nod, thinking of Handsome.

"My only hope is the fly mask. If I can get it from the drama club, Caleb will be so grateful, he'll let me visit Zed or even return Zed to me someday," Becca says. "I mean, the grandma will be happy to see Zed, but she's sick and won't be able to care for him. And Caleb will be busy training horses. So why not give Zed back to me?"

"I can think of thousands of reasons—as in dollars. Do you really think Caleb will give you a valuable zorse?" I ask, afraid her hopes are going to be crushed.

"It could happen...I hope. Returning the fly mask is my only chance to impress him. We'll get the mask from the drama club; then after school, I'll surprise Caleb with it." Becca pauses to catch her breath, then narrows her gaze at me. "You're wearing a leopard-print top."

I nod. "Do you like it?"

"Love it! But you're missing something." Becca pulls out a leopard hair tie from her backpack. "You can have this."

"I love it. Thanks," I say as I tie the strip of leopard fabric around my ponytail. With my crescent-moon necklace and leopard-print shirt and hair tie, I'm styling like Becca.

Hearing footsteps, I turn around and see Leo striding toward us. He looks more relaxed, less formal in jeans instead of black slacks.

"Seven minutes late, as promised," he declares.

"Exactly," Becca says with a grin. "Let's go to the auditorium. Sophia told me the drama club meets before and after school, so we'll find Frankie there."

"Is he the one who bought the mask from the thrift store?" I ask.

"Yeah. It was in a box of costumes," Becca answers.

As we enter the auditorium, I realize this is the first time the three of us have been together at school. I'm glad we're not hiding our friendship anymore. I don't care if anyone knows—as long as no one suspects that secret kittens brought us together.

Our footsteps echo on the polished wood floor as we walk toward the raised stage. Except for a faint murmur of voices, it's quiet. When we have school events here, it's crowded and so noisy you can't hear the person standing next to you.

I scan the tiered seats until I locate the source of the voices. Three kids sit on the raised stage in folding chairs, papers in their hands—probably scripts. Rehearsing, I guess, for the *Lion King* play. One of them is Sophia, who stands from her chair and jumps off the stage to meet us in the aisle.

"Hey, Becca and Kelsey." She runs her hand through her spiky black hair as she looks curiously at Leo. "I've seen you around but don't know your name."

"Leopold Polanski," Leo says, holding out his hand.

Sophia raises her brows at Leo's outstretched hand; then she shakes it. I can read questions in her gaze and know she's wondering why we brought him with us.

"Can you take us to Frankie?" Becca asks.

"Um...sure," Sophia says. "You said he has something that belongs to you?"

"Long story. Tell you about it later." Becca shakes her head, her ponytail swishing over her shoulders.

"Okay, but I have to warn you: Frankie can be moody and he doesn't talk much. But he's a brilliant set designer, so he's useful to have around." Sophia tucks her arm into Becca's. "Come around to the prop room."

We walk past the boy and girl rehearsing, but they're so focused on the pages they're reading aloud, they don't look up.

"You probably heard I'm going to be in our next play, *The Lion King*," Sophia tells Leo, her glitter eye shadow sparkling under the bright overhead lights. She leads us around a velvety blue stage curtain.

"I didn't," Leo says.

Sounds from the stage fade as we step through a side stage door.

"I have a leading role." Sophia waits, clearly expecting Leo to compliment her.

But Leo has slipped into the Leo Zone. He's staring up with fascination at the overhead cables and pulley system, probably calculating a more efficient system.

"It's a great role." Becca slips her arm around Sophia. "You'll make a fabulous Nala."

"Thanks." Sophia beams. "There are so many lines to learn, but I already have them memorized."

"I can't wait to see you perform." I turn to tap Leo's shoulder, so he'll stop staring at the ceiling and join the real world. "You'll go to the play with us, won't you, Leo?"

He blinks. "Why would I do that?"

"Because it's going to be amazing," Becca says enthusiastically.

Leo shrugs. "I don't go to plays."

"But I'll be in this one, so you can't miss it," Sophia says, checking him out like she's interested, which surprises me. I never think of Leo that way— although he does look really good in jeans. "*The*

Lion King is our most ambitious production ever. Frankie is super busy creating costumes and jungle sets. I told him to make my lion head like the one Nala wears in the Broadway version. Would you like to see a photo of it, Leo?"

But Leo points to a circuitry box connected to the wall. "There's a loose wire," he says. "It poses a fire risk if not repaired."

"Whatever." Sophia rolls her eyes at Leo, then points to a door marked Storage. "Frankie handles all the tech stuff."

And he'll know where the fly mask is, I think hopefully.

We enter a brightly lit room crammed with shelves, tables, costumes, and unusual props, like a life-size wooden bear, a tin man (probably from last year's production of *Oz*), animal-shaped chairs, a pink couch, and a guillotine that looks real enough to chop off a head.

The room is so crowded with props and boxes stacked to the ceiling that I can't see the walls. I don't see any sign of a kid named Frankie either and wonder if the room swallowed him.

I jump when a tall kid pops out from behind a shelf. He walks toward us in a floppy way, like his arms are made of strings. A green cap covers what looks like short black hair with a pink curl sweeping over soft puppy-dog brown eyes.

"Frankie?" I guess.

He lowers his gaze shyly and slouches like he's uncomfortable with his height. "Yup," he mumbles.

Sophia gestures to us. "Frankie, meet Kelsey, Becca, and Leo."

He nods, tipping his green cap further down his face.

"They want to talk to you, so try to act human." Sophia rolls her eyes at him. "Answer their questions, okay?"

He nods again, his cap so low now I can only see the tip of his nose. He's either very shy or antisocial.

"I hope you're not too busy to answer a few questions." Becca offers him her sweetest smile.

"I was working on a hyena head," he says. "But it can wait...I guess."

"Why aren't you working on my lion head?" Sophia complains. "It has to be finished by dress rehearsal."

"So do all the other costumes," he mutters so low I almost don't hear him. "I'm working as fast as I can."

"Alone?" Leo glances around the room with a thoughtful expression. "Don't you have anyone to help you?"

"Frankie can handle it," Sophia says with a dismissive wave. "And he has help from the stage crew on weekends. But Frankie creates all the costumes and most of the sets. I really need to get back to rehearsal. I'll leave you with Frankie. Good luck." She hurries out of the room.

I catch Frankie glaring at Sophia before his expression goes blank again. "What do you need?" he asks us.

"A mask," I answer.

"Hundreds of them around here." He shrugs. "Monsters, animals, famous faces. What kind of mask are you looking for?"

"A fly mask," Becca says.

"No insects except a spider mask with attached legs."

My skin crawls at the word *spider*. "Not a costume mask," I explain. "A fly mask is for horses to keep flies away."

"Here's a photo." Becca whips out her phone, tapping a few keys, then showing him the screen. "See, it's made of a netting and leather. Horses see great through the netting and flies can't bother their eyes."

Frankie only glances at the photo, tapping his foot impatiently like he can't wait for us to leave.

"Have you seen it?" I ask hopefully. "The mask trim is bejeweled and was part of the box of costumes you picked up from Wear-Ever Thrift."

"If you just point us in the right direction, we can look ourselves." Leo steps forward. "We'll search so you can get back to your work. I can see you're very busy."

"I am busy, but usually no one notices," he says with a genuine smile that shows a gap in his top front teeth. For the first time, Frankie looks at us with interest, not like we're pesky insects he'd like to swat away. "Okay. I'll show you the box. I haven't had a chance to sort through it yet, so it's still in my office."

"Office?" I look around at the mass of costumes and props.

"This way," Frankie says.

We follow him as he takes us on a narrow path through boxes, to the back of the room, where a few boards stacked on boxes is a table, with a laptop and piles of papers, pens, and tools on top. The wall behind the table is papered with old play flyers: *Wizard of Oz, Our Town, Frankenstein, Charlotte's Web,* and many more, most yellowed and dusty.

Becca points to a newer flyer on the wall. "There's one for *The Lion King.*"

I follow her gaze, smiling at Sophia's name. The cover art shows elaborate jungle animal costumes, some like puppets or on stilts or mechanical.

"Frankie, what are those?" Leo points at a jumble of metal poles.

"Parts for a mechanical giraffe. The poles connect to make legs with motorized wheels that will roll across the stage. But I haven't figured out how everything fits together." He points to a large white box. "Ah! There is the thrift store box."

"Can we open it?" I ask as Becca and I eagerly bend over the box.

"Sure." Frankie raises a brow. "What's the big deal about a fly mask?"

"My mother gave it away by mistake," Becca explains.

"Are the jewels worth big bucks?" Frankie wipes his dusty hands on his jeans.

"No. All fake," I say. "But it means a lot to an elderly woman because it was a gift from her husband before he died."

"She wants to wear a horse mask?" Frankie asks, puzzled.

"No." Becca giggles. "Not her—it's for her pet zorse."

"Zorse?" Frankie laughs—a deep booming sound that seems too big for his scarecrow-skinny body. "Is that even a real animal?"

"Very real and real special," Becca says. "I've had him for over six months, but now his real owner wants him—and the fly mask—back." Sighing, Becca starts digging through the donation box.

I glance over to see if Leo is going to help, but he's wandered off somewhere. Scooting beside Becca, I reach into the box. I toss aside wigs and masks and weird clothes, like a hairy vest and tie-dyed underwear. But when we reach the bottom, there's no mask.

"Drats," I mutter as we put everything back in the box.

"Maybe it's the wrong box," Becca says. "Let's ask Frankie."

We walk over to his desk (the long board propped on boxes), where he's staring at a photo of an elephant costume on the computer screen. When I tap him on his green cap, he jumps with a start. "What now?" he snaps.

"We couldn't find the mask," I say. "Is there another box?"

He shrugs. "Only one I picked up."

"But the mask wasn't there," Becca says with a flip of her ponytail. "The thrift store records listed the fly mask in the box they gave to you."

"Then you didn't look good enough." Frankie goes over to the box and tosses each costume, mask, and prop out until there's a pile on the floor beside him. When he reaches the bottom of the box, he looks up at us. "Definitely not here."

"Has anyone else opened this box?" I ask.

"Nope." The pink curl across his forehead sways with the shake of his head. "It's been sitting here since Saturday when I picked it up."

"Did anyone else touch the box?" Becca persists. "Another volunteer maybe?"

"The others left before I got the box. There wasn't anyone here...well, except—" He breaks off, an odd look crossing his face.

"Except who?" I prompt.

"When I picked up the box, I wasn't alone. But that's crazy. She wouldn't...or would she?" He looks down at the box, then back at us. "Izzy took your mask."

Chapter 12

Dizzy Izzy

"Is Izzy your girlfriend?" Becca asks Frankie.

He bursts out laughing. "No way. She's too young for me."

Since Frankie is a seventh grader like us, Izzy must be in sixth grade.

"Is she in the drama club?" I ask.

"Not officially, although she's been in a few plays. She's quite a little actress." Frankie smiles as he sits down in a night-black chair painted with silver stars. "Yup, I'm sure Izzy took it."

"But why?" Becca taps her pink-tipped nails on the thrift store box.

"She likes to hang out in here. But after I caught her playing catch with a glass Cyclops eye, I forbade her to touch the props. She never listens though and must have opened the thrift store box while I was sewing feathers on a headdress."

"We need to talk to her," I say. "Where's her homeroom?"

"She doesn't go to school here."

"Is she homeschooled?" Becca guesses.

"Not exactly." Frankie smirks like he's enjoying a joke.

"So how do we find her?" I ask impatiently.

"You'll have to talk to her mother." Leo grins. "Izzy is only three."

My mental image of Izzy shifts from a girl my age to a kid barely out of diapers. Did she take the mask home or hide it in this crowded room? My gaze sweeps over shelves, boxes, and piles of props. It'll take hours—or years!—to find a small mask hidden in this big mess.

"Sometimes I babysit Izzy. She's cute but spoiled," Frankie explains. "She loves twinkly things—*twinkly* is her latest favorite word. And when she likes something, she won't let it go."

"The fly mask has twinkly jewels," Becca says. "If I were three, I'd want to play with it too."

"Do you have her mother's number?" I ask.

"It'd be quicker to go to her classroom. Mrs. Ross isn't just my drama teacher—she teaches eighth grade English too."

"Oh, I know her. She's coolness," Becca says with shining, dark eyes. "I heard she performs scenes from each book she assigns. I hope I'm in her class next year."

"I talked to her once in the library," I add, then stop before I reveal a secret.

"She has the cutest purple unicorn tattoo on her ankle," Becca adds.

That's not her only tattoo, I think, smiling to myself.

It was only by chance I found out about the other tattoo. I was searching the school library for a modern retelling of *Romeo and Juliet* for a book report. A pretty teacher with black dreads dangling like snakes down her back offered to help me. When I told her what I needed, she recommended a book titled *Scribbler of Dreams*. As she reached to a high shelf for this book, her blouse rose up her lower back, revealing a tattoo of a red heart with a name inked inside: Diarmad Bearnard.

I couldn't stop thinking about the tattoo. So I did what I always do when I have a curiosity attack—I searched online. Mrs. Ross was born Sarah Ann Reid, married Bowen Ross four years ago and they have a daughter, Izzabella. Nothing out of the ordinary—until I looked up Diarmad Bearnard.

Wow! Thousands of fan-site hits for a handsome Scottish actor. One photo of his shirtless back showed a red heart tattoo with a name etched inside: Sarah Ann.

I printed the photo and filed it away: *secret twenty-six.*

"I'll talk to Mrs. Ross," Becca is saying when I look up from my thoughts. She's smiling gratefully at Frankie. "Thanks, you've been a great help."

"About time someone appreciated my work instead of treating me like a stage prop." He grimaces as he stands up from the painted-star chair. "I get bossed around a lot."

Becca nods sympathetically. "My mom treats me like that sometimes."

"A simple thank-you means a lot," he adds.

"Exactly," Becca says, then glances around. "Hey, where did Leo go?"

"Over here," comes a muffled reply from behind a towering shelf.

We find Leo kneeling on the floor, assembling

mechanical giraffe legs.

"How did you put the leg together so quickly?" Frankie's jaw sags open. "Those pieces are like a crazy puzzle and I can't figure it out."

"It's easy," Leo says, then proceeds to explain in technical terms that sound like a foreign language. Frankie seems to understand and asks so many questions that Leo tells us to go on without him.

As Becca and I leave the auditorium, the first bell rings.

Becca scowls. "'No time to stop by Mrs. Ross's room now. I'll have to wait till break or lunch—I just hope it's soon enough. I need the fly mask before Zed is gone."

"How long do you have?" I ask uneasily.

"Caleb said he wouldn't leave before I got home from school. He was going to check the thrift store for the mask until I told him our drama club has it. I didn't tell him we already searched the thrift store," she adds with a wry twist of her lips. "But I promised to bring it to him today."

"And you will," I assure her. "We know who has it."

"Yeah," Becca says, brightening. "Mrs. Ross is super nice, so she'll want to help. I'll talk to her during break."

Homeroom is fun now that Becca, Chloe, and Sophia include me in their whispers. As we bend our heads together before class starts, our crescent-moon necklaces shine silvery, and I feel a glow of belonging.

During my next classes, I can't focus on anything except the clock. I stare up at the wall and wish the clock hands would speed up to lunchtime.

Finally, fourth period ends. I race to my locker, spin open the lock, and grab my lunch bag. A whiff of sugary cookies trails along with me as I race through the halls.

Just as I reach the cafeteria door, a hand grabs my shoulder.

"Gotcha!"

I whirl around to find Becca giggling. "You startled me!" I accuse.

"Did you think I was the shadow dude coming to get you?" she teases.

I swat her shoulder. But she's right—that was exactly what popped into my mind.

"Come on, brave spy girl." Becca tugs me away from the crowd of kids swarming into the cafeteria. "Wait till you hear what I found out from Mrs. Ross. Let's go somewhere private to talk," she adds, leading me around the side of the building.

"Is Leo joining us?" I ask, glancing around.

"No. He texted me that he's helping Frankie, but he'll meet us after school at the bicycle rack."

"So what did Mrs. Ross say?"

Becca's face lights up. "When I told her the fly mask belongs to an elderly woman who is sick, she was really sympathetic and said we could talk to Izzy."

"Great!" I say and we high-five.

"The only problem is that Mrs. Ross doesn't think her daughter took the mask." Becca rolls her eyes. "According to her, Izzy is a perfect child who never does anything wrong."

"That's not what Frankie told us."

"Exactly." Becca nods. "Little kids love to play with things that don't belong to them. I'm sure Izzy has the mask. The hard part will be getting it from her."

"Maybe we can trade her one twinkly thing for another." I point to the yarn flower I'm wearing on my shirt. "I'm sure Sunflower Mary wouldn't mind if I offered to trade my flower for the mask."

"Or Izzy might like one of my hair ties." Becca touches her ponytail, then grits her teeth with determination. "Whatever it takes, I'm not leaving Izzy without the fly mask."

I'm determined too, but when the last bell rings, my stomach twists in knots. I've had too much time to think of everything that could go wrong. Izzy might refuse to talk to us. She may have lost the mask. She may have thrown it away.

Becca is waiting at the bicycle rack. While we wait for Leo, she shows me a map on her phone with directions to the Ross house.

"They live near downtown," I say, trailing my finger on the map. "We'll pass Sunflower Mary's house on the way."

"I wish we had time to see her sunflower garden," Becca says. "Mrs. Ross has drama club after school, but her husband knows we're coming. So all we have to do is get the mask from Izzy and give it to Caleb."

Sounds easy, right?

A few seconds later, Leo rolls up on his gyro-board. Balancing with one foot, he glances nervously over his shoulder. "Is Frankie still following me?"

"Why would he do that?" Becca asks, with a sharp glance around the school buildings and parking lot. School just let out, so kids are swarming like a human hive.

"I don't see him," I say, peering beyond Leo. "And a tall, skinny kid in a green hat would be hard to miss."

"He may not be there now, but I spotted him following me," Leo says.

"Why would he do that?" I ask.

"It's my fault." Leo hangs his head sheepishly. "I told him I was meeting you after school. I should have realized he'd be curious. He asked how we became friends, and I couldn't think of a lie."

Becca gasps. "Did you tell him about the kittens?"

"Or our club?" I ask.

"No. I didn't reveal CCSC information—which made him suspicious. When I left, I saw his reflection in a window and realized he was following me."

"We can't let him find out our secrets," I warn. "Stay away from Frankie."

"But I like helping him," Leo argues. "I promised to come back tomorrow to assemble an elephant."

"Frankie can make his own elephant," Becca says firmly as she lifts her bike off the rack. "Protecting our club is more important."

"Affirmative," Leo says with a sad sigh.

Becca and I take off on our bikes, and Leo zooms ahead on his gyro-board. Galena Park is across the street from the Ross house. Becca and I roll into the park and prop our bikes by a bench where Leo is already waiting for us.

"Target house sighted." Leo points to a boxy, two-story brick home with a huge oak tree in the front yard reaching higher than the roof.

Becca peers across the street. "Kelsey and Leo, you should be my lookouts. Izzy might be scared if we all questioned her, so it's better if I talk to her alone."

"You're our social operative," Leo agrees.

"Okay with me," I say, but I'm a little disappointed to be left outside.

"If I need anything, I'll text Leo," Becca says as she takes out her phone.

"Texting isn't covert enough," Leo tells her. "Give your phone to me."

She hesitates, then hands over her glittery, pink phone. Leo pulls out his phone from his pocket. Placing the phones side by side, he taps keys on each phone. His fingers move so quickly, I can only glimpse flashing images. Finally, he seems satisfied and returns Becca's phone.

"Our phones are synced—like a Skype—so we'll

be able to hear and see what's happening in the house," Leo explains. "Your phone is muted, so no one can hear us. Hold your phone so the camera faces Izzy and the speaker isn't covered. Like this."

Becca nods and copies his hand position; then she heads for the Ross house.

Sitting close on the bench, Leo and I stare down at his phone, which shows pavement as Becca crosses the street. She lifts the phone to a view of the front door and we hear a chime. A thirtyish bearded man with dark-rimmed glasses opens the door. He wears a navy-blue jacket over a long-sleeved shirt and jeans. Behind him, a little girl clutches a red-haired doll to her chest as she spins like a ballerina, her white-blond hair flying.

"Izzy," I guess.

Leo nods. "Subject sighted."

Izzy stops spinning to stare up at Becca with curious blue eyes; then the screen dips lower for a close-up of the red-haired doll. I recognize the cloth doll with loopy yarn curls because I have a set of Raggedy Ann books on my shelves. The stories are magical, and I love how Raggedy Ann has a candy heart with the words *I love you* tucked inside her stuffed body. Once I put a candy heart in my

Raggedy Ann doll, but ants swarmed all over her.

"Becca has infiltrated the house," Leo reports.

I glance down at Leo's phone. The screen jiggles, sweeping across a tile floor, then rising to the ceiling, then stopping on Izzy sitting on a couch.

"My wife told me you wanted to ask Izzy about a mask?" Mr. Ross says.

"It's a netted mask that keeps flies off horses," Becca explains. "It's trimmed in leather and sparkly stones. It means a lot to a sick old lady and was mistakenly donated to the drama club. We think Izzy may have borrowed it from the drama club."

"I can't imagine why she'd want a horse mask when she has a room full of toys. But go ahead and ask her while I grade papers." He gestures to papers stacked on the coffee table. "My wife isn't the only teacher in the family."

Footsteps fade off screen to be replaced with angelic blue eyes. I hear Becca saying, "Izzy, that's a very pretty doll."

"She's mine. Her name is Rayann," says a high-pitched voice.

"I liked to play with dolls when I was your age," Becca says sweetly. "Sometimes I'd dress them up. Do you ever dress up your dolls in sparkly clothes?"

The blue eyes narrow shrewdly. "Maybe."

Becca keeps talking to Izzy about dolls and clothes, leading up to the topic of the fly mask. But this little girl is too smart. She knows exactly what Becca wants—and she's not going to cooperate.

I gesture to the angel-faced girl on the screen. "She has the fly mask but she won't give it up," I tell Leo.

Leo looks at me, surprised. "How do you know?"

"From the stubborn way she said the doll was 'mine.' I recognize that attitude because I was stubborn like her when I was little. She will never give us the mask."

"So how do we get it?" Leo asks.

"We have to find it first, then figure that out."

"Oh." Leo frowns. "Where do you think she keeps it?"

"In her bedroom. I think it's that room." I point to the second story, where pink curtains flutter in a screened window. "Only how can we get up there?"

"We won't have to." Leo's eyes gleam. "My dragon drone will do it for us."

- Chapter 13 -
Dragon Flying

Leo sets down the phone, so I can't hear what's happening inside the house. We're both focused on the second-story pink-curtained room.

"I've been waiting for a chance to try out my new surveillance tool," Leo explains as he reaches for the leather pouch he carries instead of a backpack.

"A new drone?" I ask.

"Affirmative. It's so small, it makes my bird-drone look like a pterodactyl." He reaches into his backpack and pulls out a silver-winged insect.

"Cool!" The robot is tinier than a thumb. It looks so real, like it could flutter into flight if startled. But up close, I can see it's a robot—metallic with large, translucent, brown wings and glassy eyes that I guess are some sort of video camera.

"Want to see my dragon drone in action?" Leo asks as he holds a remote control in one hand and the drone in the other. He clicks the remote. Glassy eyes flash like headlights, and there's a high squeal of energy. The finger-sized wings whirl until they're spinning so fast I can't see them anymore— and then it takes off!

The dragon drone zooms over our heads and past the huge oak tree, up to the second-floor room with the open pink curtains. The glass window is open, but the screen keeps insects—even metal ones!— from getting into the room.

Leo operates the remote so the dragon drone flies back and forth in front of the window. It nearly crashes into the window screen, but Leo jerks back on the remote in time. The drone soars through leaves and has a close call with a tree branch. *Watch out!* I think but don't say, since we don't want to attract attention and a family with toddlers just entered the nearby playground.

When the tiny spy swoops back to the window, I let out the deep breath I've been holding. He made it!

"The camera is recording everything in the room," Leo explains. "When it comes back, I'll connect it to my phone, and we'll see photos of the room."

"Cool." I glance back at the phone as I hear Becca's frustrated voice cry, "Izzy, you must have seen the fly mask."

"No, no, no," Izzy says.

Stubborn little girl, I think. Then I switch my gaze back to the remote-controlled robot. The dragon drone spirals away from the window, winging its way back to us. Once it reaches the park, it hovers over our heads, then plummets like it's going to smash on the sidewalk—but Leo reaches out to catch it in one hand.

"Safe!" He hits a button on the drone, and the dragon mouth pops open. Leo takes out a dime-sized disk from the jagged-toothed mouth, then fits it inside something that looks like an electric plug attached to his phone. Izzy's whining voice coming from the phone ends abruptly as the dragon-drone data is downloaded into the phone.

When the download ends, the phone shows a view of trees and pink curtains. The drone view draws closer, up to the window screen. Izzy's room is right out of a decorating magazine. Everything is perfectly matched, from the cotton candy–pink carpet to the antique-white furniture. A princess bed with a lacy canopy, castle-shaped toy box, glass cabinet of dolls, and stuffed animals on a shelf are perfectly arranged for display, rather than toys to be played with. The only thing out of place is a Raggedy Andy doll on her purple comforter. He's propped up against pillows—but instead of wearing the usual red-checkered clothes, his cloth arms stick out through a netted vest trimmed in purple and black jewels.

We've found the fly mask.

But how do we get it?

An idea pops into my head, and there's no time to waste.

"Leo, I can get the mask, but I need you inside the house with Becca," I say urgently. "Make up some excuse to get inside."

He shakes his head. "I'm not good at lying."

"Go to the door and say you can't wait any longer for Becca because you need to go to the bathroom."

"I don't need to use the bathroom."

I reach down to the ground, rub my hand in the dirt, then smear the dirt all over Leo's hand.

"Kelsey!" He jumps away from me with shock. "Why'd you do that?"

"Now you need to use the bathroom to wash your

hands. No lying required," I say smugly. "After you wash your hands, tell Becca to keep Izzy distracted. Do *not* let Izzy go upstairs."

"What are you going to do?" he asks uneasily.

"Climb that oak." I point up. "When I reach that big branch, I'll cross it to Izzy's window. I'll pry open the screen, sneak inside, and take back the fly mask."

"That's a really high tree."

"I've been climbing trees since I was little."

"Take this." With his clean hand, he offers me his phone. The screen is back on Izzy, and I hear Becca pleading with her to show her the fly mask. "Kelsey, keep this with you, so you can hear what's going on. Good luck," Leo says, then hurries across the street.

Making sure our bikes are locked, I leave them by the bench, then cross the street to the Ross house. I take off my spy pack and hide it behind a camellia bush and look up, up, up at the tree. The tree is really, really tall. And I'm kind of short.

Still, I'm a good climber. I can do this...I hope.

The huge oak shades the yard, creating shadows to hide in as I reach for the lowest branch. It's high over my head, so I jump. I miss on the first and second tries but grab it on the third. I swing my legs up, then push myself around, so I'm straddling the branch. Standing like I'm walking a balance beam, I tiptoe along the branch until I'm close enough to reach for a higher branch. I grab and swing my feet—too far. I sail over the branch, but grab hold and land hard on my stomach. When I pull myself upright, I hear a rip. I groan at my "borrowed" leopard shirt. There's a tear down the side.

If I survive climbing this tree, my sisters are going to kill me.

But I'm not a quitter, so I keep going. I reach high for the next branch, grab, swing up, then repeat until I'm straddling the branch across from Izzy's window.

Unfortunately, this branch isn't as sturdy as the others. It wiggles as I inch out on it. I clasp my hands in front of me and move slowly.

From the phone in my pocket, I hear voices.

"Thanks for letting me use your restroom," Leo is saying.

Izzy's shrill voice pipes up. "No, I don't like dolls or playing dress up."

"What do you like?" Becca persists sweetly.

"Candy and fire engines and glitter wands."

"I make glitter hair ties like this," Becca says. "Would you like one?"

"No," Izzy snaps. And in the background, I hear Leo asking for a glass of water.

I'm about a foot from the window. A leaf flutters down and snags in my hair. When I pull the leaf out, the limb wobbles. I hold tight as the limb bends like it's going to snap—which would send me tumbling down to the ground.

Please, don't break! I think desperately.

The branch stops wobbling. I sigh with relief.

I'm just a hand reach from the window. So close! My fingertips brush the ledge. The window is open, so just a screen separates me from the room. In my old house, I sneaked into my sisters' room often, so had lots of practice prying open screens. But the branch is creaking...

I grasp the window ledge just as the branch snaps off. I hold tight by my fingertips. My feet dangle in the air.

Don't look below, I warn myself. I'm not afraid of heights—in fact, I was really good at gymnastics, until my family couldn't pay for my classes anymore. But gymnastic equipment was never this high.

Focus on the window.

The ledge is wider than it looked from below. Gripping tight, I swing one leg up, then the other.

Safe!

Slowly, I straighten till I'm standing on the ledge against the window.

From up here, I can see the street with an occasional car driving past and the park where more kids have come to the playground, their parents watching from benches. The bench we sat on is closer to the street, our bikes safely locked to a rack. Everything is in miniature from this viewpoint

I make the mistake of looking straight down to the ground.

It's a long way to fall—but falling is not an option. I can do this. I focus on the window. I shut out everything else. Queasiness fades and I'm back in control.

I don't need Leo's key spider to break into this window. Screens make it so easy, and there are no locks to slow me down (probably because they don't expect anyone to climb up to a second-story window).

I pry open one corner of the screen, then the other, until the whole screen pops out, and I push it inside the room—then follow.

The cotton-candy carpet is so soft, my feet make no sound as I walk over to the bed.

Raggedy Andy gives me a blank, button-eyed stare as I lift him and take the mask (which he wears like an apron) off his arms.

Yay! I've found the fly mask. It's made of sturdy black netting, tawny leather, and trimmed at the bottom in black and purple jewels. The purple stones sparkle like real jewels, but the smaller black stones don't even shine. There's an empty spot for the largest stone—the blue one Leo found that we gave to Caleb.

From the phone, I hear a cry from Becca, "No! Not upstairs!"

I snap to alertness. Time to leave!

I run to the window, climb out on the ledge, then snap the window screen back into place.

Getting down the tree is much quicker than going up, though it's scary reaching for the nearest sturdy branch. I climb from branch to branch until I let go with a jump.

Picking up my spy pack, I slip it over my shoulders.

I hurry across the street, holding tight to the fly mask.

- Chapter 14 -
Ditzy Dog

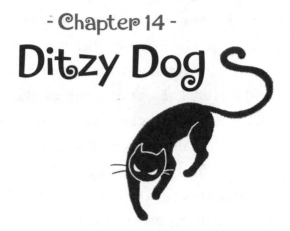

Becca and Leo join me minutes later in the park, by our bikes.

"Look!" I announce, waving the jeweled mask toward them.

"I can't believe you found it!" Becca's ponytail whips back and forth as she shakes her head. "Izzy said she didn't have it."

"Adorable little liar." I smile. "But now it's the truth, since she doesn't have it."

Leo leans close to the mask. "The jewels appear surprisingly real."

"But we know they're fake," I remind him.

"Do we?" Leo runs a finger over a shining purple stone. "I'd like to test them for authenticity."

Becca snatches it protectively from my hands. "I'm taking this directly to Caleb. He'll be so impressed," she adds with a hopeful smile. Her smile changes to a frown though when she looks closely at me. "Kelsey, your leopard shirt is torn."

"And dirty," I say with a rueful glance down.

"I'll fix it for you when we get to my house," she offers. "I still can't believe you climbed all the way up that tree. You're amazing, Kelsey!"

"We worked as a team," I say modestly, but inside I'm puffing up with pride.

"Mission accomplished." Leo jumps onto his gyro-board. "Let's go."

"I see you washed your muddy hand." I can't resist teasing him.

He grins. "Turns out I *did* have to go to the bathroom. Meet you at Becca's house." With a click of his remote control, he zooms off.

Becca and I unlock our bikes. By the time we hop on them, Leo is already out of sight. As we near the downtown area, I get an idea.

"Let's turn at the next street," I tell Becca.

"Why?"

"Just come with me," I say mysteriously.

She follows me on a side road I rode down a

few days ago. Yellow blooms burst into view, and I glance over to Becca, who is slowing her bike to stare with delight.

"Sunflower Mary's garden," Becca exclaims.

I nod at the same time Mary herself hobbles out from the porch and waves us over.

"So good to see you again, sweetie," she tells me. "And you brought a friend. She's wearing a sparkly necklace like yours."

"She's a Sparkler," I say.

"Hello, Mary." Becca waves. "Remember me?"

The wrinkles around Sunflower Mary's eyes deepen as she studies Becca. "Oh my, yes. But you've grown taller than me and so pretty with your father's dark hair and mother's sunny smile. Shame they split up. Do you still live with wild animals?"

Becca nods. "Not all of them are wild. I share my bedroom with a miniature goat and two sweet dogs."

"A goat in your room? Now that's strange," says the strangest woman I've ever met. "Do you still have your flower?"

"I wish. But that was years ago." Becca props up her bike on the sidewalk and walks over to the garden. "Your flowers are so gorgeous. How do you grow them so big?"

"I never reveal my secrets. I'm sure your friend understands about secrets," she says, glancing over at me with a knowing look. But she can't know about my notebook of secrets.

Or does she? I wonder. When I met Mary yesterday, she admitted knowing more than people realized. Living near busy downtown streets, she can observe people going to jobs, appointments, or socializing with friends. She knows my father and Becca's parents. She probably knows more about Sun Flower than anyone else—which means she might be able to solve one of our mysteries.

"Mary, can I ask you something?" I say carefully.

"Sure thing, sweetie. What?"

"I found a pen—I don't have it with me—but it's blue with a logo from a business I'd never heard of: Desert Sun Train. Does that sound familiar?"

"We're near hills not the desert, and there aren't any trains here—except the model trains in Cody Lancaster's basement. But that's just a hobby, not a business."

"Model trains?" I consider this, then shake my head. "The word *train* on the pen isn't clear and there's a faded spot for another word after it."

"So it could be a word similar to train," Becca adds. "Like grain or brain."

"Which doesn't help us at all," I add with a groan.

"Why the fuss over a pen?" Mary's shrewd eyes sharpen. "Where'd you find it?"

"On the ground," I say cautiously because she's too curious (like a grown-up version of me). Before she can ask more questions, I glance at my watch. "Wow, look at the time; we have to go."

Becca nods. "Mom must be wondering where I am."

"Your mother was a sweet child—you look a lot like Renee. Shame about your father...but not all romances are meant to last. Tell your mother she needs to get out more and listen with her heart. And take these with you." Mary pulls out two yarn flowers from her skirt pocket and hands them to Becca. "For you and your mother."

"Thank you," Becca says as she clips the sunflower to her shirt. "I won't wash this one in the machine."

"Wear it proudly," Mary says in a crackly voice.

Becca doesn't have her backpack, so I offer to let her put the second yarn flower in my spy pack. "It'll be safe there until you get home," I offer.

"Good idea," Becca says as she hands her mother's flower to me.

I sling my spy pack off, onto the sidewalk, then zip it open. A bejeweled strap from the fly mask sparkles on top.

Quick as a blink, Sunflower Mary swoops down to grab the mask. "And what is this pretty trinket?" she says, holding it up so it shines in the sunlight.

"Not a trinket—a fly mask for horses," Becca says with an uneasy glance at me.

"I've ridden lots of horses but never saw such a sparkly fly mask." Mary shakes her head. "These purple and black jewels must be worth a fortune."

"They're fakes," I explain.

Mary squints at the mask, then rubs her finger over the shimmering stones. "The black stones look like pebbles, but these purple ones gleam like sapphires. Much too fancy for a horse."

"He's a zorse, not a horse," Becca corrects. "And he is very special."

I pluck the mask from Mary's hand. "We have to go," I say as I zip the mask and yarn flower inside my spy pack.

We thank her for the yarn flowers and hop back on our bikes and pedal away.

I feel Sunflower Mary's gaze on me, but I don't turn around.

I pedal faster, not even slowing as I turn the corner.

"Watch out!" Becca cries.

A small brown dog darts across the road in my front of my front tire. I slam my brakes and jerk the wheel away from the dog. Skidding, I grip tightly, so I don't fly off my bike. Tires squeal as my bike stops.

The brown dog pads calmly down the road as if nothing happened.

"Are you okay?" Becca cries, rolling up beside me.

"Shaky but relieved. Thanks for the warning. I didn't even see him until he was right in front of me!" I wipe sweat from my forehead.

"He was running fast, but now he's stopped on that lawn." Becca points a few houses down across the street.

I follow her gaze to where the dog is lifting his leg on a bush.

"I've seen that dog before," I say, surprised. "His name is Ditzy!"

"How do you know him?" Becca asks.

"His picture was on a missing pet flyer."

"Poor lost dog," Becca says. "If he keeps running

in the streets, he could be hit by a car. We have to catch him."

"But if we go after him, it could take so long, Caleb might leave."

"The dog is more important than a fly mask."

"But Caleb is probably already at your house."

"He can wait." Becca looks worried. "I'll text Leo, so he can tell Mom and Caleb I'll be late. Speedy Leo is probably already at my house. He'll tell Mom and Caleb to wait for us and that we found the fly mask. Come on. We have a dog to catch!"

Ditzy isn't a big dog—a dachshund. But he's fast and catching him isn't easy. We chase him on our bikes, then jump off when he darts into an empty lot. I can run faster than Becca, so she stays with the bikes while I take off after the dog.

When he stops to sniff a bush, I lunge forward with my arms outstretched.

"Gotcha!" I cry as I pounce on him.

He squirms but wags his tail, so I know he doesn't mind being held. He's heavy though, and I'm panting by the time I return to Becca. She has her phone out and the screen shows the Humane Society's page for missing pets.

"Ditzy has been missing for two days. I'm calling

his owner now," Becca tells me as I grip the dog's collar tightly. He's still squirming but not as much. He sniffs Becca's leg, wagging his tail excitedly. He probably smells the menagerie of animals from Wild Oaks Sanctuary.

I keep hold of Ditzy while Becca talks on her phone. The owner lives on the other side of town. We wait in the empty lot until she arrives in an SUV with a little boy about Izzy's age strapped in a car seat in back. As soon as the woman steps out of the car, Ditzy jumps inside and licks the little boy. Laughing, the kid hugs his dog and thanks us. Izzy could learn some manners from him.

The mother insists we take a twenty as a reward. I tuck the bill into my pocket. As the CCSC decided, half of any reward money will go to our kitten fund, and the other half will be donated to the Humane Society.

Finally we hop back on our bikes. We don't talk as we roll past downtown, then up the steep hill to Becca's home. But I know Becca is worried that Caleb didn't wait and has already left with Zed. I don't think he'd go without the mask, but you can never predict what grown-ups will do.

When we ride into Becca's driveway, Caleb

Hunter's horse trailer is right where he left it. There's no sign of his truck, which he's been using to drive back and forth. I breathe out a sigh of relief.

Leo rises up from a porch chair and rushes over, frowning. "You're too late."

"No, we aren't." Becca points to the trailer. "Caleb hasn't left yet."

"Actually, they have." Leo tucks his hands into his pants pockets.

"They?" Becca asks curiously, swiveling her gaze from the horse trailer to the pasture. "But Zed is grazing in the field and the trailer is still here."

"Caleb left with your mom in her car," Leo says.

"Why would they leave together?" Becca twirls the end of her ponytail around her fingers. "Where did they go?"

"Out to dinner," Leo answers. "On a date."

- Chapter 15 -
Real or Fake?

"My mom and Caleb!" Becca hands fly to cover her open mouth.

I'm shocked too, although now that I think about it, Caleb and Becca's mother have been getting along really well. But I never expected them to *like* each other.

"Weird, huh?" Leo chuckles. "According to my calculations, 29 percent of perfect first dates lead to marriage. Not great odds, but if it happens, then Caleb Hunter will be your stepfather."

"Shut up!" Becca snaps. "My mother is not ready to date. She's only been divorced for three years."

"My dad just moved out and he already has a girlfriend," Leo says calmly. He's okay with his parents splitting up because his house is peaceful now, not a war zone.

But Becca is the opposite of calm, as if her emotions are at war. With reddening cheeks, she slams her hands on her hips to glare at Leo. "I repeat—my mother is *not* ready to date. Not Caleb or anyone."

I put my arm around Becca. "It's just a date. They're not getting married."

"But if they did, you wouldn't lose Zed," Leo says cheerfully. "He'd be part of your family."

"No, no, and *no*." Becca stomps her foot on the gravel driveway. "I don't want that cowboy for a stepdad. He is definitely not Mom's type."

"They're just sharing a meal," I remind her.

"A dinner *date*!"

Leo squints at her. "I don't understand why you're so mad."

"I am not mad...I'm just not happy." Becca takes a deep breath, then blows it out. "But eating together doesn't mean anything romantic."

"They're also going to a movie," Leo says.

"A movie!" Becca's dark eyes widen in horror. "But Mom never goes to movies. The last time I asked her to take me, she said she was busy. Too busy for me but not for *him*? And they'll be gone for hours, so I can't even give Caleb the fly mask."

"He said not to wait up for him," Leo adds. "He'll be back in the morning."

"Seriously?" Becca throws up her hands. "After we worked so hard to get the mask, Caleb doesn't even care."

"He said he was grateful," Leo says. "He wants to thank you before he leaves."

Leaves with Zed, I think sadly.

"Also Caleb said to take extra care of the mask." Leo turns to Becca. "He suggested you keep it in a safe place, away from animals, until the morning."

"Your mother must have told him you sleep with a goat," I can't resist teasing.

"And that ferrets run loose in our house. But I live on an animal sanctuary, so where is it safe to keep the mask?" Becca complains with a rueful gesture from the house to the pasture. "There are animals everywhere."

"But only two small kittens in our clubhouse," I say, thinking quickly. "We can keep it inside our snack container. The plastic lid is kitten proof."

"Good idea." Leo grabs his gyro-board from where it's propped against the porch. "We should check on the kittens anyway."

"Yeah, but first I have to fix Kelsey's shirt." Becca points to me, then turns back to Leo. "You go on ahead and take care of the kittens. Kelsey and I will meet you there in about twenty minutes."

"Agreed." Leo hops on his gyro-board and zooms down the road, toward the wooded hill above Wild Oaks Sanctuary.

Becca leads me into a back room crowded with all kinds of stuff—animal beds, boxes, an ironing board, a treadmill, and a sewing machine. She loans me one of her shirts to wear while she cleans my shirt with a rub-on stain remover and sews up the rip. When she hands the leopard shirt back to me, it looks brand-new.

"You're the best friend ever," I say, then my cheeks burn with shame. Did I just call Becca my best friend? I didn't mean it that way, but she might think I did. I wish I could stuff the words back in my mouth.

But Becca doesn't notice. She's staring at a framed photograph of her mother next to the sewing machine. Her mother is laughing while riding a camel. She's in her twenties, like how Becca will look in ten years.

A short while later, Becca is quiet as we bike up the hill. But I can tell by her dark expression that she's thinking troubled thoughts. Is she worrying about her mother dating Caleb or Zed leaving in the morning? Probably both.

Leo's already inside the clubhouse, putting away the cat food cans into the cupboard, when Becca and I walk through the door. It's a cloudy day, and with the shutters closed, the shack seems darker, less inviting than usual. But the kittens happily munch their food like they haven't eaten in days, although it's only been since morning.

While Becca cleans the litter box, I check the water bowl. Yuck—there's a dead fly floating in the water. I scoop out the dead fly, then pour in fresh water.

Usually after the kittens are fed, Leo works on the broken grandfather clock. But he's tilting his head in his "thinking" way.

"Can I see the fly mask?" he asks me.

"Sure." I unzip my spy pack and hold out the bejeweled mask.

Leo takes it over to the table and carefully spreads it flat. He pulls his phone from his pocket and snaps photos of the mask. Tucking his phone back into his pocket, he leans down to closely examine the mask, rubbing his finger over each stone. I read his lips as he counts the black stones and larger purple stones inset into the leather trim. He touches the empty setting where the blue stone we gave to Caleb fits.

"What are you muttering, Leo?" Becca asks, her hands on her hips.

"He was counting the stones," I answer since Leo is too focused to reply. "Now he's counting backward."

Leo ignores both of us, moving his lips silently. Twenty, nineteen...thirteen, twelve...When he reaches zero, he lowers the mask.

"What was all the counting about?" I ask him.

"I was executing the minute test to determine the authenticity of the stones."

"Authenticity?" I laugh. "Caleb told us they're fakes—although the purple ones look real." I glance down at the yarn flower attached to my shirt and remember how dazzled Sunflower Mary was by the jewels. She really believed they were real.

Leo lowers the fly mask, then touches the stones. "They're warm. Genuine amethysts stay cool but a fake will heat up to forehead temperature. Also, amethysts are deep purple with different hues, but these stones lack depth. They're definitely fakes."

"We already knew that," Becca says with an eye roll.

"I'm being thorough," Leo insists. "I want to give all the stones a glass test."

"What's that?" I ask.

"A simple procedure of rubbing a stone against glass to see if it scratches."

"Not going to happen." Becca plucks the mask from Leo's hands. "You might break a jewel or rip the netting. Caleb wants me to keep this safe and that means no tests."

Leo frowns as Becca puts the fly mask inside the plastic food container and seals the lid shut.

"Let's discuss CCSC business," I suggest, trying to lighten the tension between Becca and Leo. I sit at the table and wave for them to come sit beside me. "Becca, we still haven't told Leo about the dog."

"What dog?" Leo pulls his chair close to the table.

"The lost one we returned today," I say proudly. "He ran out in front of my bike."

"He was superfast," Becca adds. "It was hard to catch him."

"But we did it together," I say with a grateful look for Becca. "And we didn't expect a reward—

the flyer didn't offer one—but the owner insisted we accept this." I reach into my pocket and give Leo the twenty since he's our club treasurer.

"Good work." Leo reaches for a metal lockbox he keeps on a high shelf and tucks the money inside. "What breed of dog was it?"

"Dachshund. I'll find his photo," I say, flipping through the stack of lost pet flyers I keep in my spy pack.

Becca and I talk fast, interrupting each other, as we describe how we caught Ditzy. I tease Becca about how she fell trying to climb a fence, and she points to the stains on my jeans from stepping in a hole. We start to laugh and even Leo joins in. Our conversation shifts to other club topics, like when to make a vet appointment for the kittens, treasury expenses, and studying more missing pet flyers so we'll be ready next time we see a stray animal.

I glance at my watch. An hour has passed—I need to get home.

But my kitten scampers over and swats at my shoes—her way of asking me to pick her up. I cuddle Honey's soft fur against my cheek. Her purring is like my favorite music, and I hate to put her down, but I do it anyway.

As I straighten up, I see a flash of green and pink out the window.

I gasp. "No way!"

"What's wrong, Kelsey?" Becca exclaims, coming up beside me.

"Did you see something?" Leo asks.

"Not something—someone." I point at the window and shake my head in disbelief. "That drama kid Frankie was spying on us!"

- Chapter 16 -
Spying on a Spy

Quick as a lightning flash, Leo rushes outside. The door bangs behind him.

When I jump up to follow, Becca pulls me back. "Let him do this alone. If it was Frankie, this is between them."

"It *was* Frankie," I say with certainty.

"Did you see his face?"

"No, but I saw his green cap and pink curl. Leo told us he thought Frankie was following him."

"But all the way out here?" Worry lines crease Becca's forehead. "Why would Frankie do that?"

"He knows we're hiding something."

"And now he knows what we're hiding—kittens in our clubhouse." Becca groans.

"Maybe we should have kept our friendship a secret," I say. "We're so different, it makes kids wonder why we're together."

Becca points to my Sparkler necklace. "Not so different anymore."

I nod but feel like a fraud. Wearing sparkly accessories and animal-print clothes is Becca's style, not mine. There's a tug on my shoelaces, and I bend over to scoop up Honey. Kittens are something Becca, Leo, and I all have in common.

"How long do you think Frankie was following us? Do you think Frankie followed us to Izzy's house?" Becca scoots her chair closer to mine.

"I hope not." I gnaw on my lower lip. "If he did, he saw me climb into Izzy's window and take the fly mask."

"And he followed Leo here," Becca says miserably. "Now our clubhouse isn't a secret."

"Frankie could ruin everything for us," I complain with a fist-pound on the table. The noise startles my kitten, and she springs off my lap.

Becca scowls. "Frankie is a sneaky, creepy, spying snake."

"And Leo's friend," I say with a sigh.

We play with the kittens while we wait for Leo.

The kittens are so cute, tumbling over each other as they chase a string. But I'm sick with worry. What if Frankie tells other kids about our clubhouse? Leo has to convince him to keep our secrets.

Can a sneaky snake spy be trusted?

Minutes later, Leo returns with mud stains on his slacks—and he's alone. He sinks into his chair, breathing hard like he's been running for miles.

"I almost caught up with him, until I tripped and fell over a rock." He winces and points to the rip on his black pants. "When I got up, he was gone."

"You're bleeding." Becca tears off a paper towel strip and hands it to Leo.

"Thanks." Leo wipes his knee, then tosses the soggy towel into the garbage. "I couldn't see his face, but from the back, he sure looked like Frankie. But he didn't stop when I called his name. Why would he run from me?"

"He's a lying snake." Becca twirls the end of her ponytail. "I liked him when I first met him, but now he's enemy number one."

I frown. "He had no right to spy on us."

"But it's okay for us to spy on other people?" Leo counters. "That's hypocritical."

"Hippo-what?" Becca squints at Leo.

"Hypocritical is when you criticize someone for doing something you do," Leo explains. "Why is it wrong for Leo to spy but okay for us?"

"We're solving mysteries," I answer.

"Maybe Frankie is trying to solve the mystery of us," Leo says defensively. "I trust him. He'll keep our secrets if I explain how we found the kittens and that our goal is to help all animals. He's probably headed back to the drama storage room. I'm going after him."

"I'll go with you," Becca offers.

"We'll all go," I say, even though I should go home. But my curiosity is stronger than my fear of getting into trouble.

As I pedal quickly to keep up with Leo, I wonder about Frankie. Did he follow us because he was curious, or was it something more sinister? Is he a psycho stalker?

Helen Corning Middle School is a sprawling school with covered hallways connecting outdoor class-rooms. Usually it's noisy and bustling with activity, but two hours after the final bell, it's like the school has gone to sleep for the night. Our footsteps echo as we near the auditorium. The door is propped open, and I hear raised voices—shouting, then a scream.

But it's only a drama rehearsal, I realize when we see Mrs. Ross up on the stage, directing three students including Sophia. When Mrs. Ross gives us a friendly wave, I feel a little guilty because I sneaked into her daughter's room. But I only took back the mask that "perfect" Izzy stole.

We go through the side door that leads to the storage room. Leo doesn't bother to knock. He strides purposefully into the room and up to Frankie's desk.

"Nice surprise." Frankie looks up at us with a grin, dropping a pen and pushing aside the paper he'd been writing on. "I didn't expect you back so soon."

"I doubt it's a surprise," Leo says in an accusing tone. "We saw you."

"Saw me where?" Frankie reaches up to pull his green hat down, so it covers up his pink curl and shades his eyes.

"You know," Becca adds. "Kelsey caught you spying through the window."

"And I chased you through the woods." Leo narrows his blue eyes. "Why did you follow me?"

"Follow you?" Frankie's eyes go wide. "You're joking, right? I haven't gone anywhere."

"I saw you." I fold my arms folded over my chest.

"Tell us the truth," Leo says almost like he's pleading.

Frankie frowns. "You're calling me a liar?"

"Kelsey and I both saw you," Leo insists.

"Couldn't have been me," Frankie says firmly. "I always work here after school."

Could I have been wrong? I wonder. I saw green and pink and assumed it was Frankie. Am I sure it was him?

"Ask the drama kids and Mrs. Ross," Frankie says, standing from his desk. "They'll tell you I haven't left this room."

"Okay, we'll talk to them," Leo says stiffly.

"I'll go with you. Just a sec while I clear away this mess," Frankie tucks away pens, paper clips, and Post-Its in a drawer.

"I don't like a messy desk either," Leo admits.

"We have a lot in common." Frankie looks directly into Leo's face as he rips up a paper and dumps the pieces into the trash. "I thought we were friends."

"I did too," Leo says, his sad eyes showing hurt.

We weave through crowded shelves to the door. As we step out into the hall, Becca turns to Frankie.

"I need a restroom," she says. "Is there one close by?"

"Over there." Frankie points across the hall.

"I'll wait for you," I tell Becca, but she shakes her head.

"Go ahead. I'll catch up."

Frankie's arms are tight at his sides, not relaxed. He marches ahead of us like a soldier going off to battle—grim and determined. Leo follows with hunched shoulders.

Is Frankie innocent or a sneaky snake? I wonder. The face at the window looked like him, but what if I'm wrong? Whoever it was knows CCSC secrets. He spied on our clubhouse, saw the kittens, and even watched Leo hide the treasury money.

"Frankie never left the building," Mrs. Ross tells us a few minutes later. And the drama kids vouch for Frankie too, even Sophia.

We leave the stage and head for the storage room.

"Told you," Frankie says. "I'm not your spy."

"Then who is?" Leo rubs his head. "The guy I chased was tall, thin, and wore a green cap like you."

"Did you see his face?" Frankie asks.

"No," Leo admits.

"It could have been any tall guy wearing a hat like mine."

"I'm sorry." Leo hangs his blond head. "I should have trusted you."

"Yes, you should have. But you can make it up to me by helping out with the costumes," Frankie says with a grin. "You were genius assembling the giraffe. Want to get started on the mechanical elephant?"

Leo agrees quickly, smiling like a huge weight has rolled off his shoulders. Poor guy doesn't have many friends—maybe just us. He and Frankie seem a little alike—smart but socially awkward. It's cool if they become friends.

Yet I'm uneasy. If Frankie isn't the spy, then who is?

Leo goes into the storage room with Frankie, and I start to follow until Becca pops up beside me and whispers, "Let's get out of here. I have something to tell you."

"We already know Frankie's innocent," I say with a heavy sigh. "The drama club—even Mrs. Ross—said he never left the building. I was wrong about him."

"Maybe," she says with a mysterious smile.

We walk through the theater aisles toward the exit. As we push open the auditorium door, the wind tosses our ponytails. We head for the bike racks. When I glance over at Becca, her dark eyes sparkle brighter than her crescent-moon necklace.

"What's up with you?" I ask as I unlock my bike.

"Nothing."

I glance at her curiously. "You're smiling too much."

"Am I?" Her smile widens.

"I get the feeling you know something I don't know," I guess.

She lowers her voice. "I didn't buy Frankie's innocent act, so I did a little snooping."

"In the bathroom?"

"I didn't go there. That was a ruse, as we say in spy talk. I searched Frankie's office and found important evidence." She reaches into her pocket and shows me a handful of paper pieces.

"Looks like trash not evidence."

"And you call yourself a spy," Becca teases. "Didn't you notice how weird Frankie acted about cleaning his desk and ripping a paper? Why rip it up—unless he's hiding something."

I rub my chin thoughtfully. "It did seem strange."

"Highly suspicious," Becca says. "So I collected

all the paper pieces and hid them in my pocket. I'll tape them together like I did with the letter in your spy game."

"Excellent! Too bad I don't have tape with me. I'll have to add it to my spy pack. But I do have this." I dig into my spy pack for a baggie and offer it to her. She stuffs the paper pieces inside, then we head for my house since it's the closest.

When Mom sees me walk in with a friend, she gets all excited like I've never brought a friend to our apartment—which I haven't. Mom also notices my shirt.

"Doesn't that belong to one of your sisters?"

"Um...maybe," I say, smoothing over the leopard fabric.

"It looks great on you," Mom says. "I'm glad someone is finally wearing it. Did your sisters give it to you?"

"Uh...not exactly."

"Well, they should," Mom says with a chuckle. Instead of criticizing me, she offers to return it to my sisters' closet.

"Go change before your sisters get home," Mom says with a conspiratorial wink. "Becca can wait here with me."

When I come back, I'm wearing a sky-blue sweatshirt over comfy jeans. Mom and Becca sit close together on the couch, chatting like they've known each other for years instead of a few minutes.

I give Mom the leopard shirt, then turn to Becca. "Come on. Let's hang in my room. We have that project to work on," I add with a meaningful look.

"Oh, yeah. The *project*." Becca pats her pocket where she has the letter pieces. She turns back to my mother. "Anytime you want a tour, I'll set it up."

"Thanks," Mom says. "I've really missed being around animals."

I grab Becca's hand and escape to my bedroom.

"What tour?" I shut my door and lock it.

"Wild Oaks Sanctuary. Your mother might become a volunteer. She said she has lots of free time since her florist job is only part-time and she enjoys working outside. She talked to me like a friend, not bossy like my mother does. Your mom is coolness."

I smile, pleased and little proud of Mom. "Dad's the diva in the family, and Mom is the peacekeeper. They balance each other out."

"You're lucky," Becca says with a wistful sigh. And I guess I am. My family has financial problems, but at least we're together.

Becca opens the baggie I gave her and spills paper pieces onto my desk.

"You'll need this," I say, then hand her a roll of tape.

There are about thirty pieces of paper, and Becca swiftly arranges them into place like puzzle pieces. The uneven pieces don't lie flat, but Becca manages to smooth them out with bits of tape and fit them together. She must have been practicing because she's really good at this.

Finally all but one piece—a jagged corner—is in place, a colorful image of jungle animals emerging. I find the missing piece on the floor and carefully stick it in place. I hold the tape, ripping off strips until Becca has the paper pieces together.

"It's only a flyer for *The Lion King* play," Becca says, disappointed. "I thought it would be a letter or coded message."

"You did a great job of piecing it back together."

"But it tells us nothing about Frankie. I was just so sure..." Becca's voice trails off as tosses the taped flyer toward my trash can. But she misses and it sails down to the floor. Neither of us bothers to pick it up.

"I was sure I saw Frankie too," I confess. "But it must have been someone else."

"Someone who now knows all about the CCSC," Becca adds grimly.

I groan, my gaze drifting down to the floor to my shoes, which are scuffed and mud stained. I'm thinking how I should wash my shoes when I notice something odd about the flyer.

"Look!" I grab the paper and point. "When it fell to the carpet, it flipped over and there's writing on the back."

Becca and I read it together.

Chapter 17

A Puzzling Clue

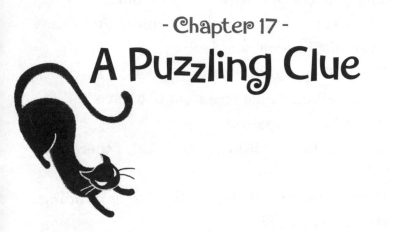

Frankie has terrible handwriting.

It's hard to decipher the words scribbled on the bottom of the paper. At first glance I think they're just doodles until a few words jump out at me:

Wild

Club

Cats

Another word looks like it begins with "san" and has a *t* in the middle…Could it be sanctuary? *Wild* could be for Wild Road or Wild Oaks. Either way this paper proves Frankie *was* at the Skunk Shack. He wrote down what he saw; then, when we almost caught him, he ripped up the evidence.

But Becca pieced it back together.

"I bow to your puzzle mastery," I say as I hand back the paper. "This proves Frankie *did* spy on us."

"Why did the drama club—even Mrs. Ross—say he never left?" Becca wonders.

"Maybe they didn't know," I guess. "They saw him go into the storage room but not leave."

"How did he sneak out?"

I rub my chin for a moment. "Could there be a back door?"

"There must be." Becca nods. "Large buildings usually have lots of exits."

"So Frankie left through the back door, then returned the same way, and no one knew he left," I guess.

"What a sneaky snake." Becca scowls.

"He was convincing," I say. "He should be acting in the drama club."

"As a villain," Becca adds bitterly.

I stare down at the scribbled words, a trail of guilt adding up. "Frankie wrote down what he saw. He followed Leo to Wild Oaks Sanctuary, then climbed up the hill and through the trail to our clubhouse, where he spied in the window."

"Exactly," Becca says with a triumphant snap of her fingers. "Now all we have to do is confront him and make him explain." She sits on the edge of the bed, a worried look creasing her face. "But how do we tell Leo?"

"Oh" is all I say because I don't have a better answer.

I sit on the bed beside her, our legs dangling over my carpet. Leo seemed happy to work on the costumes for Frankie. I've never seen Leo so relaxed. He's going to be so disappointed when he realizes Frankie lied.

"Do we have to tell Leo?" I ask Becca.

"Yeah." Becca blows out a heavy sigh. "But it can wait."

"We'll tell him tomorrow," I agree, and we shake on it.

Becca isn't in a hurry to return to her empty house, so we study for a science quiz. We work until the aroma of homemade corn bread and spicy chili is too strong to ignore. My parents invite Becca to join us, and suddenly an ordinary night becomes a party.

My family—even my sisters who usually look down on middle schoolers—are fascinated by Becca's stories of living on a wild animal sanctuary. She tells us about a dog with the hiccups, being sneezed on by the zorse, and a duck that fell in love with a cat.

It's dark by the time dinner is over. My parents offer to drive Becca home, and I tag along with them. After putting her bike in the rear of our SUV, I sit in the backseat beside Becca. My parents have the radio blasting '80s songs, so Becca and I have to lean close to hear each other.

"I really like your family," Becca confides.

"And they like you too. Usually my brother can't wait to leave the table, but he stayed for Dad's blueberry cheesecake."

"It was delish! Your dad's an amazing cook. It's cool your mom might volunteer to help at the sanctuary. She's easy to talk to—the opposite of my mom," Becca adds wistfully. "Mom used to be fun—before Dad left."

I remember Mrs. Morales saying how hard it was to run a sanctuary alone. I've never asked Becca about her father and only know he's living in Washington. "Maybe your mother is lonely," I say.

"How could she be lonely when she has me? Yeah, we argue, but I help her out a lot. She doesn't need anyone else."

"Are you sure?" I ask softly. "You're not home that much with school, the CCSC, and the Sparklers."

"Mom isn't home tonight," Becca complains. "She's with that cowboy."

We don't say much after this. I hum along to the song coming from the front seat radio. I watch Becca twirling the end of her ponytail and realize I'm twirling mine too. Streets, houses, and cars blur by as I try to think of something to say that has nothing to do with her mother, Caleb, or Zed. So I talk about the Sparklers.

"Any new ideas for the fund-raiser booth?" I ask.

"Only old boring ideas. We'll probably do face painting again."

"But even Tyla admits that wasn't profitable. Your hair ties are so pretty; they would sell like crazy," I say, reaching up to touch my leopard hair tie. "I'm wearing mine the same way you wear yours."

She gives me a startled look. "Why did you change your hairstyle?"

"Because yours looks so great on you. I admire your creative style."

"But your style is *you*," she says so loudly my mother glances at us from the front seat. "You're already coolness. And you have a great family. I hardly ever see my dad, and when I try to talk to Mom, we end up shouting."

"So don't talk—listen. Give your mom a chance."

"She won't give me a chance." Becca shakes her head.

"Sure she will, if you give her your big smile that wins everyone over. People naturally like you. I envy that. Before I started hanging out with the Sparklers, no one even knew my name."

"I did," Becca says. "You sat behind me in homeroom, and I admired how smart you were. Whenever the teacher asked you a question, you got it right without coming off like a smarty-pants. I wanted to get to know you, but whenever I turned around to talk, you looked away."

"I did?" I ask, surprised.

"I thought you didn't like me, so I gave up trying to talk to you."

I can hardly believe this. I think back to the times I stared at the back of her head, wishing she'd talk to me. And to think she was wishing the same thing! If we hadn't rescued kittens together, we wouldn't be friends.

"Once I tried to dye a pink stripe in my hair like yours," I confess.

"Don't try to be like me." She takes my hand and looks directly into my eyes. "I like the way you are and others do too. Wear your hair loose, put on comfy jeans, and go back to sitting with your other friends at lunch if you want."

"I don't want to—I really like the Sparklers."

"Even Tyla?" Becca asks doubtfully.

"Well...I'm working on it. But you're right. I'd rather wear jeans and T-shirts minus all the sparkles—except my necklace." I reach up to trace the smooth crescent shape.

"Just be Kelsey," Becca says as the car slows to drive under the archway announcing Wild Oaks Sanctuary. She unfastens her seat belt, then leans over to whisper in my ear. "I think you're the coolest girl ever."

As I'm getting ready for bed that night, I can't stop smiling.

Becca thinks I'm cool.

This is better than every awesome holiday and birthday present combined. And I really do like who I am—not a sparkly girl, just plain Kelsey

Case. If I'm in a ponytail mood, I'll wear one of Becca's hair ties. But otherwise, it's back to comfy T-shirts and jeans and my hair loose around my shoulders. I'm not going to be like anyone but me starting tomorrow.

Tomorrow, I think with a jolt, *Zed will be gone.*

And we didn't solve the mystery of who abused him.

As I slip into my pajamas, question marks whirl though my head. We found the fly mask but we don't know who dropped the blue pen I labeled "Evidence A." Did the shadow dude plan to rob the thrift store? Or was it a homeless person looking for a place to sleep?

That night, I toss and turn like the fairy-tale princess troubled by a tiny pea beneath her mattress. Only my troubles feel boulder sized. Who abused Zed? Why did Frankie spy on us? Will my father ever find a job? Who tried to break into the thrift store? What do the words on the blue pen mean?

Desert Sun Train…train, brain, rain, stain…

Questions whirl, spin and torment me until—

"That's it!" I jerk up in my bed.

I glance at my illuminated clock flashing 3:14 a.m.

It's pitch-dark outside, but a light bursts bright inside my head. Clues add up and point to one person.

But I need proof.

Tossing a robe over my pajamas, I race from my room into the living room and power up the computer. I pull up a search engine and type a name.

A few links come up, but they don't match my suspect. I try a search combined with the word *horse*.

Bingo!

There is it!

I think back to when Becca first told us Zed's owner was coming to take him away. She suspected that Caleb Hunter was a fraud and didn't really own Zed. But Leo's web search confirmed Caleb Hunter did indeed live in Nevada, was the grandson of Zed's owner, and trained horses at D. S. Ranch.

D. S. Ranch, I ponder. *Why does that ranch sound so familiar?*

The more I look at D. S. Ranch, the more my brain tingles. Could D. S. stand for Desert Sun? *Desert Sun Train* — the words on the blue pen! Only it's "training," as in someone who trains horses. Not a sand and dune desert, but a high desert of sage and chaparral.

Hello, Caleb Hunter: suspect number one.

But what's Caleb's motive? Is he more interested in Zed or the fly mask? He was eager to leave with Zed—until he found out the fly mask was missing. When Becca's mom told him the mask had been donated to the thrift store, he said he'd wait till Monday to look for it. Yet he didn't wait. He hid his identity like a thief and tried to break into the store. Only we scared him away, and he tripped over a turtle and dropped his blue pen. If I'd seen him the next day I bet he would have been limping.

Why go to so much trouble for a bejeweled fly mask? The answer is obvious—the jewels must be real and worth thousands. That would explain why Caleb is so eager to find the mask but not why he lied to us. Did he think we would keep the mask for ourselves if we thought it was valuable?

But Caleb wasn't the only one who said the jewels were fakes. Leo's authenticity test proved the jewels weren't real. How can I find out the truth? I can't believe anything Caleb says, and his grandmother is too ill to ask. Who else might know?

I go back to the computer and skim through the information on Caleb Hunter until my gaze stops on the name Carol Hunter-Bowling.

Caleb's sister.

Hunter-Bowling isn't a common name, so it's easy to search for her. She's a real estate agent and her website gives a business address, phone number, and email. I can't call in the middle of the night, but I can send an email.

Do I address it to Miss, Mrs., or Ms. Hunter-Bowling? A husband isn't mentioned, so I can't tell if she's single, married, or divorced. I settle on just her first name and hope that's okay.

Now what do I write? I need to let her know right away I'm a friend and not spammer. I should also say I'm sorry her grandma may be dying, but tactful like, not a blunt, "Is your grandma dead yet?" And I want to ask if the fly mask jewels are real.

I start off with "I like your zorse," then hit delete and replace it with "My friend has your grandma's zorse." Hmmm, still doesn't work. So I rewrite again, adding three words. Next I type, "I hope your grandma is feeling bitter." Oops, typo. I change "bitter" to "better." I add two more sentences and it seems perfect—until I realize I called the zorse "Zed" instead of "Domino." Another rewrite and I'm done.

Dear Carol,
My friend has been caring for your grandma's
zorse. I hope your grandma is feeling better.
She'll be happy when your brother returns
Domino. I have some questions about the fly
mask. Can you call or email me?

Sincerely,
Kelsey Case

I add my phone number, then hit send.

When I crawl back under my covers, I fall into a
sleep so deep that I don't wake up until I hear Mom
calling my name.

"Kelsey, Kelsey!" I open one sleepy eye and see
my mother peeking into my room. "Why aren't you
up yet?"

Slowly, I sit up in bed and stretch out my arms.

"You have a phone call," Mom says, holding out
the phone to me. "It's Becca, and she sounds upset.
Let me know if there's anything I can do for her."

"I will." I jump out of bed and take the phone.

"Becca, what's up?" I say into the phone as the
door thuds shut behind Mom.

"Something terrible has happened," Becca says,

her voice cracking. "I got up early and went to the Skunk Shack—"

"The kittens!" I interrupt. "Are they okay?"

"They're fine. But when I went to get the fly mask, it was gone." I hear tears in her voice. "The fly mask has been stolen."

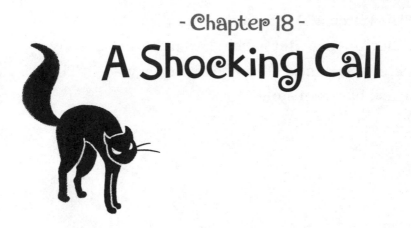

Chapter 18

A Shocking Call

"Mom!" I shout as I rush down the hall. Her bedroom door is open, and she's standing in front of her free-standing mirror, holding up a blue pleated skirt and matching vest.

"Is Becca okay?" Mom drops the clothes on her bed and comes over to put her arm around me. "When I talked to her last night, she seemed stressed."

"She's not hurt or anything, but she's having a crisis and wants me to come over."

Mom frowns. "I can't drive you because I have an important appointment."

"I can get there quickly on my bike." I look up at her hopefully. "Can I go?"

"Of course. If Becca needs you, you have to go to her."

Then you know what my mother does? She calls my school to say I'll be late.

"You're the best," I say and give her the biggest hug ever.

I consider calling Leo, but I'm sure Becca already texted him about the theft. He's probably on his way to her house.

Hurriedly, I slip into the first pair of jeans I find and put on a comfy green T-shirt. As I reach for my backpack, I notice the yarn sunflower on my dresser. I grab it for luck. I need all the luck I can get today.

Slinging my backpack over my shoulder, I race downstairs. Dad is flipping bacon chocolate chip pancakes (a combo that's surprisingly yummy), and he insists I take one. I curl one in my hand like a pancake-burrito and start for the door.

It's chilly and wind flings my hair around my face. As the door shuts behind me, I hear the phone ringing, but it's hardly ever for me, so I hurry down the stairs for the apartment's bike rack.

I'm unlocking my bike chain when I hear Mom shout my name. I look up to find her leaning against the second-floor rail and waving the phone.

It must be Becca! I think anxiously as I race back up the stairs. *Has she found the fly mask?*

When I put the phone to my ear, I hear a strange woman's voice.

"Is this Kelsey Case?" She sounds about Mom's age.

"Yes." I bite my lip as I glance down at my watch. "I'm in a hurry…"

"So am I," the woman says firmly. "I just read your email."

"Email?"

"You sent it last night…well, this morning," she adds. "I'm Carol Hunter-Bowling."

"Oh!" I almost stumble down the stairs. "Caleb's sister."

"Unfortunately." Her voice drips bitterness. "I was shocked by your email. I thought Domino was dead."

"He's very much alive. Didn't your brother tell you?"

"We don't talk," she says bluntly. "You wrote that Cal was bringing Domino home to our grandmother?"

"Yes." I smile, imagining the happy reunion. "My friend Becca—she lives at the Wild Oaks Sanctuary— has been caring for Ze…I mean…Domino for over six months, and he's doing great. His scars are healed and Becca can even ride him. She really loves him."

"I'm glad someone there does, because my brother doesn't."

I switch the phone to my other ear to make sure I heard right. "Caleb told us he was heartbroken when Domino ran away."

"Of course he told you that," Carol says sarcastically. "Cal is very good at saying what people want to hear."

"What do you mean? Caleb cares a lot about the zorse. And he's worried about his grandma. He almost cried when he spoke about her being so sick…maybe dying."

"Grandma was in bad shape after the stroke, but now she's getting around on a walker and the doctor says she can move back to the ranch soon. She's reluctant to go home though, because Domino isn't there."

"Caleb is bringing him back today," I point out.

"I'll believe it when I see it," Carol says doubtfully. "I don't know what scheme my brother is up to, but I don't trust him—especially with the zorse."

"I don't understand. He showed us photos of your family with the zorse, and everyone looked happy together. He trains horses, so he must love animals."

"Cal *is* good with horses, and he's a decent horse trainer. But a zorse is *not* a horse and can't be forced to learn." Her voice rises with anger. "Grandma warned Caleb over and over not to use harsh training techniques on Domino. But my brother couldn't get that through his thick head."

"He tried to train Zed...I mean, Domino?"

"Yes, even after Grandma ordered him to stay away from Domino. My brother is not a terrible person, but he has a terrible temper. And his pride couldn't take being bested by an animal. He tried to force Domino into submission with brute force. I don't blame Domino for fighting back."

Even though I'm afraid to ask, I do anyway. "What happened?"

"My brother whipped Domino."

I gasp, remembering Becca describing how Zed had been beaten. "No! Caleb was the one who did that? But I thought Zed ran away because he was spooked by an ambulance, then was hurt during the months he was missing."

"The ambulance did spook him, but Cal did all the hurting. Since I was riding to the hospital with

Grandma, Cal said he'd stay at the ranch and take care of the zorse."

Caleb also told us he would "take care" of Zed. I shudder at the new terrible meaning of those words.

"I wouldn't have known what really happened if Grandma didn't have a security camera on the corral," Carol continues. "Unfortunately, it was weeks before I checked the video. By then, I thought Domino was dead and didn't want to add to Grandma's grief by telling her what Caleb did. I confronted Caleb though, and threatened to turn the video over to the police if he ever hurt another animal." Her voice cracks. "I still have nightmares about that video. It made me sick to watch that poor zorse whipped until he fought back and bit my brother."

I think back to the ugly scars on Caleb's arm. He told us a horse tossed him into barbed wire. But he was lying...about everything.

"Why did Caleb come to Wild Oaks?" I say, gripping the phone tightly. "If he hates the zorse, why drive hundreds of miles to return him to your grandmother?"

"He has no intention of returning the zorse," Carol says furiously. "I'm sure of it."

"But he's picking him up this morning."

"That scares me because my brother never forgets a grudge. Domino bit him, which is a blow to his pride. Cal is out for revenge."

I gasp. "Do you think he's going to hurt Zed?"

"He already did once," she says sadly. "I'll do what I can to stop him. I'm getting in my car now, and I'll be at Wild Oaks Sanctuary in a few hours. Tell your friend to stall my brother until I can get there."

I hurry over to my bike. "I'm going to Becca's house right now."

"Good," she says, sounding relieved. "No matter what happens, do not leave my brother alone with the zorse."

"I won't," I promise.

As I click off the phone, my thoughts race faster than my pounding heart.

It's hard to imagine Caleb, the sweet-talking cowboy, beating an animal. Becca was suspicious of him until he showed the video of Zed/Domino as a foal. But her first impression was right, and we never should have trusted him.

My hands shake as I dial Becca's cell number. It rings over and over until her voice mail invites me to leave a message.

"Becca, why aren't you answering?" I rant at the phone, "Zed is in trouble! I have to warn you about Caleb! Don't let him take Zed!"

I stare at the phone anxiously. If I can't talk to Becca, I should try her mother—except I don't have her mother's number. I could look up Wild Oak Sanctuary's number, but that would mean losing precious time by going back inside the house and searching for a phone book or waiting for our outdated computer to power up.

It's quicker to bike to Becca's.

Hopping on my bike seat, I pedal faster than I ever have in my life. It's not until I'm blocks away that I realize I'm still holding the house phone. Oops. It's just an extension anyway, not the main phone. When I stop at an intersection, I toss it into my backpack on top of my English literature book.

My legs pump up and down, wheels spinning so fast my spokes are a blur. I think back to when we met Caleb. Becca was suspicious of him. But he was just so nice...maybe too nice? When he showed us the video and told stories about his family, even Becca liked him.

He fooled all of us.

Was he the one who stole the fly mask? I wonder

as I hit a bump in the road and bounce up and down on my seat. I was so shocked by Carol's call, I forgot to ask her if the fly mask jewels are fake or real. Not that it matters now. The mask is gone. Caleb is the most likely thief. But why take the mask when we were going to give it to him? Unless he wanted to make sure no one knew he had it. But how could he know where Becca hid it?

Downtown rushes by in a blur of cars and businesses. I practically fly up Wild Road, my throat aching from breathing hard. *Faster*, I urge myself. I have to get there before Caleb comes for Zed. It won't be easy stalling Caleb, but Becca, Leo (if he's there), and I will figure something out. Mrs. Morales might help too — if she believes me. She did just go out on a date with Caleb, maybe even kissed him. Yuck.

Hurry, hurry! I tell myself. But Wild Road is steeper near the top of the hill and my legs ache. I grip the handlebars tightly as I push myself faster.

At the crest of the hill, I pass the dirt road we usually take when we go to the Skunk Shack and continue on to the long driveway into Wild Oaks Sanctuary. A wooden sign etched with animal drawings welcomes me to the sanctuary.

Gravel crunches beneath my tires as I near the last curve in the driveway and see the red, pointed top of the barn.

I cross my fingers that Caleb's horse trailer is still parked by the barn. It'll be even better if the truck, which Caleb has been using to drive around town, isn't there.

Turning the corner, I see the trailer, but it's not parked by the barn.

It's not parked at all—it's moving!

Pulled by Caleb's white truck, the large horse trailer slowly backs up, turning around to pull out of the driveway. Through a trailer window, I glimpse a black-and-white tail.

Caleb is leaving with Zed!

I watch in horror as the truck moves in slow motion, wheels backing up, turning, straightening, then rolling forward.

Where are Becca, Leo, and Mrs. Morales?

I want to scream for help. But screaming would attract Caleb's attention and let him know I've found out about his lies.

Exhaust puffs from the truck. I smell the acrid odor of diesel. In seconds, the truck will pass me on the road then drive away—with Zed.

I'm the only one who knows Zed is in danger.

But what can I do?

I hear Carol's warning in my head: "No matter what happens, do not leave my brother alone with the zorse."

"I won't," I vow with grim determination.

No time to find someone to help—it's all up to me. Dropping my bike between bushes bordering the driveway, I duck down low and creep around the bushes. I wait until the horse trailer is parallel to me, hoping to jump into the back and let Zed out. But the back is shut tight with a heavy steel latch.

There's no latch on the tack room door though.

Running to the side of the trailer, I yank it open.

And I jump inside.

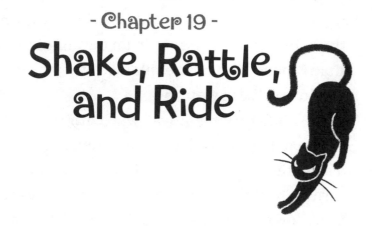

- Chapter 19 -
Shake, Rattle, and Ride

This is either the stupidest or the bravest thing I've ever done.

I'm being rattled in a giant tin can that smells strongly of leather and hay. The metal floor beneath my feet shakes. Around me, boxes, bottles, saddles, bridles, cinches, and hanging lead ropes sway and rattle. I grab on to a shelf so I don't topple over, not that's there room to fall. The small tack room is like a closet on wheels.

Now what do I do? I thought there would be an inside door leading from here to the horse stall, but nope. I can hear thumps from Zed moving around, but there isn't even a window to see him through. The walls around me are solid metal.

Why didn't I think before I jumped?

The smart move would have been to find Becca or her mom. But they could have been anywhere— the house, the pasture, or in an outbuilding. By the time I found them and explained everything, Caleb would be miles away with Zed.

Now he's driving miles away with me too.

The horse trailer leaves the gravel driveway for a smoother paved road. Wild Road, I realize as we turn right, then coast downhill toward downtown Sun Flower. The rattling has lessened, but my fears are growing.

I need to get out of here *now*.

Grabbing the handle, I push at the door. It gasps open with such a fierce gust of air that I'm thrown backward. My shoulder bangs into a metal shelf. I'm surprised my shoulder doesn't hurt until I realize I'm still wearing my backpack and it cushioned me like an reverse airbag. The tack room door creaks on its hinges, back and forth, until a swift gust of wind slams the door shut. Metal shakes so violently, I'm tossed off my feet.

I reach up to steady myself and grab a handful of hay from a large bale perched over my head. The truck lurches. The hay bale tips over, crashing down on me.

My world is eclipsed by a dark-yellow shade of panic.

Choking, hurting, buried in hay, I try to push upward and struggle to breathe. Hay is in my mouth and my hair, and itching my skin. Finally, I push aside the bale and stagger to my feet. I can breathe again, although I'm a little dizzy and feel like I might vomit.

Must. Get. Out.

But we've picked up speed, and I'm afraid to try opening the door again.

Don't freak out, I tell myself. *Calm down and think logically.*

Caleb is probably headed for Nevada, which is over a hundred miles away. He has to stop somewhere along the way, right? Either for gas or food or to use the restroom. When he stops, I can escape. But that would mean leaving Zed.

I come up with a plan to rescue us both. When the truck stops, I'll wait till Caleb is busy, then unlatch the back trailer and go after Zed. I'll untie him, then lead him out of the trailer. We'll find someplace to hide and wait for Caleb to drive away. I'll find a security guard or store clerk, and beg to use the phone to call for help. By the time Caleb realizes he's pulling an empty trailer, he'll be miles away and Zed will be safe with me.

Okay, there are a few problems with this plan, but it's the best I can do while stuck in a vibrating, hay-filled room. I'm jostled between saddles and ropes and shelves of horse equipment, making staying on my feet a challenge. Whenever Caleb changes lanes, I'm tossed to one side and have to grab on to a shelf for support. While my backpack is a great cushion, it makes keeping my balance hard.

I wiggle one arm out of the backpack at a time. The pack slips down with a thud to the hay-sprinkled floor. If only this were my spy pack. But it's not, so it has no lock picks, flashlight, or other spy tools. All I have are textbooks, pens, pencils, notepaper, gum, a pair of striped socks, two quarters, a granola bar, and the totally useless house phone. If Becca or Leo were locked inside a tack room, they'd whip out their cell phones and call for help.

At least I won't starve, I think as I rip open the granola bar.

As I chew, I mentally map out where we're going. We turned right onto Wild Road, so we should be driving past downtown Sun Flower. I imagine the businesses we pass: O'Hara Realty, Blooming Florist, the bank, and a gas station—the only gas station for thirty miles until the freeway.

I bite my lip and hope, hope, hope he'll turn into the gas station. I know the clerk, Mr. Chang, because he used to work with Dad until Café Belmond closed.

But instead of slowing, the truck picks up speed. Caleb must have a full tank. I'm stuck here until he gets hungry or needs a restroom. Drats.

As miles and minutes rattle by, my fear grows.

Instead of imagining my escape, I sink to the floor with a sense of doom. What will happen if I'm still trapped here when Caleb reaches his destination?

I huddle against the metal wall, not sure if I'm shaking because of the vibrations from the trailer or because of my fears. I huddle in a ball against the bale of hay, my arms wrapped around my bent knees.

If Caleb isn't going to return Zed to his grandmother, where is he headed? If he's after revenge, like his sister thinks, he won't hurt Zed in a public place. He'll drive somewhere remote, where no one can hear Zed's cries.

What will Caleb do if he finds me?

Jumping to my feet, I look around desperately. If there were a window, I could wave to attract attention. But there's only the solid steel door. I rub my elbow where it's sore from my last fall. I'm afraid to try the door again, but it's my only way out.

I reach a shaky hand for the handle.

Whoosh! Wind pushes against the door like an invisible wall. But I push hard as I turn the handle and blink into bright daylight. I'm careful not to open the door all the way, only a few inches. I look down and pavement rushes by. Hay swirls a cyclone from my feet to my face, like a swarm of itchy bees. Straw flies up my nose, and I sneeze so hard I almost fall backward.

The truck swerves right and picks up speed. My heart jumps into my throat as I realize we're on the freeway.

Slumping down to the floor, I try not to cry.

Okay, I'll admit I cry a little. But when I dry my eyes, I feel stronger. I may be alone in here, but I have friends and family who are probably already looking for me. Becca will know I'm in trouble if she checks her phone messages or finds my bike. She'll tell her mother, who will tell her friend Sheriff Fischer. They might even think I've been kidnapped and put out an AMBER Alert.

All I have to do is to wait for rescue.

But what if Becca doesn't check her phone? No one may notice my bike because it's hidden in the bushes. And my school won't check on me because Mom told them I was going to be late. My mother will think I'm at Becca's. Becca will think I went to school. By the time anyone misses me, I'll be across the state line.

Guess I'll have to rescue myself.

If Becca were in my situation, her cell phone would connect her with instant support from a network of friends. Leo would figure out some techno-clever way of transmitting an SOS to authorities.

But me?

Listening and watching are what I do best. I think back to news reports of people trapped in car trunks who escaped by kicking out taillights. I'm trapped in a steel cage, speeding over fifty miles an hour. If I jump out the door, I'll be a kid-sized splatter on the freeway.

Still, if I can get the door to stay open, I can attract attention by waving for help.

I turn the handle and push hard. Air rushes into the tack room. I lean my arm out as far as I can and wave frantically. Unfortunately, the tack room door is on the right side of the trailer, and since large vehicles keep to the right lane, the only living creatures to look my way are random cows.

I hear cars roaring passed in the left lane. I can't see them, and they can't see me. I'd have to lean out dangerously far to be seen by the vehicles behind us.

What if I poked something out the door that would attract attention?

I look around the tack room and only see scattered hay from the tossed bale, saddles, and other horse tack. My backpack! I have paper and pens inside. I could write an SOS message.

Ripping a piece of paper from my notebook, I write in large letters: HELP!

I find a piece of rope on the floor and poke a hole in the paper then wind the rope through the hole. I hold the rope in one hand and inch the door open with the other. I'm careful this time not to let the door open too far.

This is going to work! I think excitedly.

I lean further, dangling the paper from the rope...
Whoosh!

The wind snatches the paper, slams the door,

and I'm left holding an empty rope. Not only is my message gone, but I'm also guilty of littering.

Where's the highway patrol when you need them?

Hooves clang on metal from the other side of my wall. Zed must be getting anxious and scared. Poor guy. I know how he feels.

"Zed, I'm here to help you!" I call out just as the trailer hits a bump and lurches.

I'm tossed backward, slamming into a saddle, the breath knocked out of me.

When I can breathe again, I inhale leather and swallow disappointment.

But I won't give up.

Rubbing my shoulder, which will probably be a dark rainbow of black and blue tomorrow, I slowly get back to my feet.

I take inventory of the tack room: a bag of oats, a hay bale, bridles, wire, ropes, and a whip hanging from a wall. Hmmm...the whip would dangle out through the door further than a rope. But its dull brown color won't attract attention. I need something colorful enough to alert the world that there's a girl (and a zorse) trapped in here.

As I glance down, I spy something sparkly. Sunflower Mary's yarn flower is pinned to my shirt. It's small but glitters as bright as sunshine. I get a crazy idea.

I use the piece of rope to tie the sunflower to the end of the whip. I wind some wire around it too, so the wind won't snatch it away like it did with the paper. The flower is so bright, it shines even inside the dim tack room. Outside, the yellow yarn will glow like a golden SOS.

Balancing carefully, so I don't fall backward again, I open the door. I grip the handle firmly since I'm being rocked and knocked with each bounce of the trailer.

I reach my arm holding the leather whip out the door. It's a tricky balancing act, especially when the wind whips through the crack of the door and hay swirls into my face. I don't pull back, not even when hay flies by my eyes. Gritting my teeth, I focus on the flopping end of the whip, where a glittering yarn sunflower dangles.

It's so pretty, shining golden like a jewel. I blink away straw and hold the whip up high. I hope someone in a car behind us will notice the waving sunflower.

When I hear the first honk, my hopes rise.

A second honk blares from a car passing on the

left. Wind makes my eyes water, so I can hardly see the whip in my hand. I hold tight as hills rise into piney mountains.

The whip starts to slide through my fingers. My arm muscles burn. I can't hold on much longer. The trailer rocks to the right, and I stumble. Steadying myself, I lift my arm as high as I can, so the small sunflower flies like a golden bird. It doesn't glitter as much now though, and a strand of yarn dangles. Golden petals unravel until there's no sparkle, only a tangled trail of yellow yarn.

The wind swirls the yarn away.

I pull in the whip and the door bangs shut. Sagging to the ground, I rub my aching arms and wipe my stinging eyes.

I hope for more honks, but there's only the steady rush of traffic as we drive further away from rescue into the Sierra Nevada mountains.

The truck suddenly slows into a sharp right. I'm tossed sideways, but since I'm already on the ground, there's nowhere to fall. The road is no longer smooth. Have we left the freeway? I peek out the door and don't see any other cars, only dense woods.

Not good, I think with a pit in my gut. The road grows bumpier, and there's no sound of traffic.

After what feels like forever, the trailer slows to a stop.

Must get out of here! I think, grabbing the door handle hard. I look down at my other hand and realize I'm still holding the whip. If I have it, Caleb can't use it on Zed. So I keep hold of it.

Looking around, I see nothing except a wild forest of pines. No houses or buildings. We're cut off from civilization on a dirt road in the woods. Remote areas like this are where bodies are buried and never found.

I hear the creak of the truck door opening.

Footsteps crunch on weeds.

Caleb is coming.

Chapter 20

Whipped

Hide! I look around desperately for a hiding spot, but the tack room is too small. I push open the door and jump to the red dirt. We're on a rough road in a clearing between rising pines. If I can make it to the trees, I'll be safe.

Footsteps crunch from the truck, heading to the trailer.

No time to run for the trees—only to hide.

I dive underneath the trailer. Sharp rocks and prickly weeds scratch my skin as I crawl on my hands and knees, slipping into the shadow of a large tire.

Boots stomp into view. I hold my breath, motionless, like I'm glued to the tire. Please don't let him see me!

Peering out cautiously, I watch Caleb step up to the tack room door. He yanks open the door, then disappears inside the room. The trailer above me creaks and groans with footsteps. I remember what I left behind—my backpack with my name written all over my homework. He'll know I was there, but he won't know I'm hiding beneath his feet—unless he looks under the trailer.

I have to get out of here!

Before I can move though, a country song blasts. A phone ringtone, I realize. The music abruptly shuts off, and I hear Caleb speaking. His words are muffled, so I can't understand what he's saying until he leaves the tack room and jumps down to the ground a few feet from my hiding place.

"Better reception out here," he says. "Now what were you saying?"

I can't see his face, only his shiny, black cowboy boots, which move dangerously close to me.

"I'm on my way," Caleb barks out as if in a hurry. This must be his real voice, not the fake drawl he used when he was sweet-talking Becca's mother. "Some fools were honking at me, so I pulled off the road to check my tires. But everything looks all right."

He bends over to poke a front tire. I huddle in a tight ball behind a back tire.

"Nothing wrong with the truck or trailer," he says. "I'll get back on the road and deliver the zorse soon."

I watch Caleb's boots take a few steps, then stop inches from my hiding place. I don't dare breathe.

"What you do with the zorse after I deliver him is your business," Caleb adds with a savage chuckle. "Strap him in a harness to a kiddie ride and make him walk in circles all day or put him on display at a freak show. He's not good for much else. He may be part horse, but he's stubborn like a mule and too dumb to train."

He's too smart for you, I think.

"Of course, my family is fond of him." Caleb's tone slows to a drawl. "But my grandma is too sick to care for him, and she needs medical care that costs more than she can afford. I'm selling him to help her out."

Help yourself out! I think angrily. What a liar! Caleb doesn't care about his grandmother or he would have told her Zed was alive. He only cares about the money. And I'm sure he won't share it with his grandmother.

"The zorse is rare and worth twice my asking

price. Pat yourself on the back because you're getting a great deal." I strain to hear as he walks around to the rear of the trailer. "Got it all in cash?...Sounds good...See you after I take care of the zorse."

Take care of the zorse.

I gulp at the menace of those words.

Caleb's boots turn the corner to the rear trailer door. A metal latch clangs open.

"Back out beast," he orders.

Hooves clatter like Zed is kicking. Caleb jumps out of the way and swears.

"Try that again, and I'll give you a whooping worse than last time," Caleb threatens.

I'm holding the whip and Caleb isn't. But that won't stop him from hurting Zed. I hear a slap, then a shrill whinny. The trailer shakes as Caleb forces Zed out of the trailer. Black-and-white striped legs skid reluctantly down the ramp.

Leaning out from behind the tire, I watch Caleb tie Zed to a metal loop attached to the trailer. Zed tosses his mane, then head-butts Caleb so hard the cowboy stumbles backward.

"Want to play rough, do you?" Caleb's laugh is a mean sound. "You'll regret it when you feel the sting of my whip." He turns on his boot heels toward the tack room.

A door creaks open, and I hear Caleb muttering to himself.

"Where is that...Hey, how did this get here?" Caleb says loud enough to make me squirm because I know he's found my backpack.

Oh no! I think in panic. If Caleb finds me, he'll realize I overheard his phone conversation. How far will he go to stop me from exposing his crimes?

Time to get out of here!

If I run into the woods, Caleb will never find me. I'll climb into a tree or duck behind a rock. I could hide until Caleb drives away—but that would leave Zed alone with Caleb.

I promised Carol I wouldn't let that happen.

Trembling under the trailer, I'm sure I'll be discovered. But the only sounds come from the distant hum of traffic and wind rustling through trees. No clomp of boots. Even Zed has quieted.

Then I hear Caleb.

"I'm a skilled tracker," he says as if talking to himself or maybe he's on the phone again. I can't see his face, only his boots as he steps down from the tack room.

"I can hunt down any animal—or human— by following prints." Caleb's voice has an eerie calmness. "Sneaker prints are easy to spot, especially when they're fresh."

Not a phone call. He's talking to me.

"I know you're under the trailer."

I say nothing.

"You might as well come out, Becca."

Wrong girl, I would say if I wasn't too scared to speak.

"No reason to hide from me. We're friends, right? I'm right fond of you and your mother. You can trust me. I just want to help you get back home, where you belong."

He steps closer to my hiding place.

"I reckon you're afraid I'm angry because you sneaked into my trailer." His voice softens. "It was wrong, but I don't hold it against you. I did fool things when I was a kid too. You have nothing to fear from me."

Tell that to Zed. I grip the whip tightly.

"You probably heard me on the phone. Now don't you worry about the zorse. He's going to a mighty fine home. My poor grandma has gotten worse and won't ever be able to ride again. She's so sick, she'll die soon without expensive medical care." He breaks off with a fake sob. "The money from selling Zed will save her life."

If I hadn't talked to Carol on the phone, I might have believed this story. But I know he's only saying what he thinks I want to hear. Should I pretend to believe his lies? I don't think he'll hurt me. What did Carol say about him? Oh yeah—that he wasn't a terrible person; he just has a terrible temper.

"Come on out, Becca. Your mother will be worrying about you. You can use my phone to let her know where you are."

I hold my breath as he steps closer.

"Little girl, I don't have time for games."

This is not a game for me or Zed.

"Do I have to drag you out?"

Silence is my answer.

"You trespassed into my trailer," he accuses with rising anger. "You broke the law, but if the cops find you here, they'll think I kidnapped you. I'm not going to jail because of some fool child. Now get out here!"

Zed's hooves stomp, and he lets out a harsh whinny.

"Shut up, you stupid beast. This isn't about

you—at least not yet." Caleb bends over and peers beneath the trailer. "Get out, little girl!"

I wiggle in the dirt to hide by an opposite tire.

"Hey! You're not Becca!" His face is upside down as he hangs over to stare at me. "You're that other girl. And what are you doing with my whip?"

"Making sure you don't use it on Zed again," I say, then wish I'd shut up when his eyes go all hard and mean.

"You think I only have one whip?" he says.

Whirling around, he stomps back to the tack room.

I didn't see a second whip, but I'm not waiting here to find out.

I scoot out from the trailer, then rush over to Zed. He nuzzles his soft head against me. I glance nervously over my shoulder, but Caleb is still clattering inside the tack room. I have to hurry!

"Zed, when I take off your rope, run fast," I say urgently, hoping he'll understand. "You'll be safer in the woods like last time you ran away. I'll find you when he's gone."

He whinnies softly, his dark eyes shining at me with trust.

I work on untying the lead rope from the trailer.

But the knot is twisted and tight. I almost laugh when I realize there's an easier way to free Zed. I reach up for the end of the rope around his neck and unfasten the metal clasp. The rope falls to the ground.

"Hey, get away from that zorse!" Caleb shouts.

"Run fast!" I give Zed a push on his flank, but Zed doesn't budge.

And Caleb is running toward us—with a bigger whip in his hand.

I'm stuck between a stubborn zorse and an angry cowboy.

"Stay back!" I shout, standing protectively in front of Zed.

I lift the whip and put all my fear into snapping it.

Crack! The sound startles me so much I gasp.

Caleb just leans back with a laugh. "Not bad for a first try," he says, chuckling. "But a little girl like you can't whip me."

"Stay...stay away!" I lift the whip again but instead of snapping it flip-flops like a harmless jump rope. "Don't touch Zed."

"I'm not going to hurt him. It's just, he's so stubborn, I need the whip to get his attention."

"You're the one who hurt him," I accuse.

"I didn't mean to, and I feel bad about that. He attacked me, and I was just defending myself. See these scars from where he bit me?" Caleb sticks out his arm, lifting up his shirtsleeve so I can see the red scars. Not from barbed wire like he first said, but from the sharp bite of teeth.

"He only attacked after you beat him," I say, sure this is true.

He narrows his gaze at me. "You can't prove anything."

I purse my lips and give another floppy flip of the whip.

"That whip's too big for you to handle," Caleb scoffs. "Give it to me and move away from that beast."

"Run, Zed!" I push him, but he still won't leave.

Caleb advances, his whip rising large and threatening in his strong hand. "Stand aside or the zorse will bite you too."

Zed kicks up dirt, turning his head toward Caleb.

"I won't let you hurt him," I retort, flinging my arms out protectively across Zed.

"Out of the way, little girl. I need to get the zorse back in the trailer."

Caleb steps closer, the whip raised high.

I look into Zed's dark eyes and remember Becca saying that only people he trusts could ride him. "Trust me," I whisper to him.

He's shorter than a horse, but it's still a tall jump to his back. Caleb's whip cracks so close, air slices over my head. I grab Zed's mane with both hands and fling myself up on his back. Twining my fingers in the silky zorse hair, I hold on tight.

"Get down, you fool girl!" Caleb thunders.

Zed bares his teeth at Caleb but instead of biting, he spins on his hooves and rears out with a mighty back kick. I glance over my shoulder to see Caleb stumble. He steadies himself and lifts his whip. Snap! Air whooshes by my shoulder. Zed whinnies as if in pain. Has he been hit?

"Go, go, go!" I shout, straddled across the zorse's back.

And we're off!

It takes all my strength to hold on to Zed, zorse hair flying in my face. I cling to his mane as we gallop down the rough dirt road.

"Go to the woods, not back to the highway!" I can hardly hear my own words over thundering hoof beats.

My fingers slip, so I hold tighter. I dig my knees

into his sides. Trees whirl by, and I struggle not to fall. The roar from the freeway draws closer.

When I hear an engine, fear jolts through me. Is Caleb coming after us in his truck?

But the sound isn't behind us—it's coming from a black-and-white vehicle heading toward us.

We gallop toward the flashing red and blue lights.

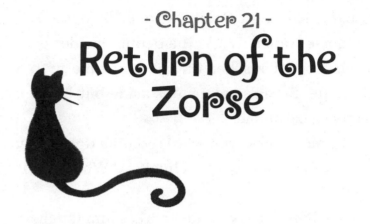

- Chapter 21 -
Return of the Zorse

I'm shocked when Becca's mother steps out of the sheriff's car. She rushes over to me, and I slip off Zed into her warm hug.

"Kelsey, I'm so glad we found you!" Mrs. Morales gently pushes a stray hair away from my face. "Are you okay, honey?"

I nod, trying to figure out why she's with the sheriff and a deputy. I recognize Sheriff Fischer, a solid man with shoulders so broad, they strain against his dark-blue uniform. We met briefly when the CCSC helped catch a pet-napper. He's all business, but his dark eyes are kind.

Sheriff Fischer confers with his deputy, a college-aged, skinny guy named Phil Harmon (Becca once teasingly called him Philharmonic). Deputy Phil strokes his stubble as he talks with his deputy. His gaze is sharp on Caleb, who shifts nervously by the horse trailer. While the deputy strides over to Caleb, Sheriff Fischer turns toward me with a gentle smile. Becca's mom steps aside but keeps a protective gaze on me.

"Last time we met, you were rescuing dogs. Now it's a zorse," he says with a chuckle. "What will it be next?"

"An elephant," I say, which makes him laugh.

"You have a passion for animals like your mother."

"You know Mom?"

"Not well, but I'm going to know her better soon. We just spoke on the phone, and she gave me permission to ask you a few questions."

"You can trust the sheriff," Mrs. Morales adds, nodding. "I've known Chad since high school, and he's a good guy."

"Thanks, Renee." He smiles and she blushes, then glances away.

"I have a good idea of what happened, but I still need to ask you an important question." Sheriff Fischer is so tall, he has to kneel down to talk to me. "Did that man force you to go with him?"

I stare at the shining, star badge on his uniform, and my mind jumps back to when I was five and a police officer asked a similar question. I lied because I was afraid of getting in trouble for hiding. But I'm not afraid now.

"Caleb didn't know I was in his trailer," I admit, honesty making me stronger. "He's not a kidnapper, but he's an animal abuser. I was afraid he would beat Zed again if someone wasn't there to stop him."

Zed nuzzles me while I explain what happened, beginning with the phone call from Carol Hunter-Bowling, her warning not to leave Caleb alone with the zorse, hiding in the tack room, and what I heard Caleb say on the phone.

"I know it was wrong to hide in the trailer," I finish. "But I had to help Zed. Look! Here's a red mark where Caleb just whipped him. And it would have been much worse if I hadn't ridden away with Zed." I turn to Mrs. Morales, imploring. "Caleb plans to sell Zed. You can't let him!"

"I'll do what I can," Mrs. Morales promises.

She takes the sheriff aside for a whispered talk. I can't hear what they're saying, but I can lip-read well enough to know Zed won't be going anywhere with Caleb soon. Not today—and hopefully not ever.

"I have an important appointment to make," Caleb gripes. "I don't have time to go anywhere with you! And it's my zorse. I can do whatever I want with him. I have the papers to prove it."

"We'll sort this all out at the station," Sheriff Fischer says gruffly. "My deputy will ride with you in your truck."

Everything is a blur after that. Mrs. Morales sits with me in the backseat of the sheriff's car. She holds me warm against her, and I doze off.

When I wake up, we're driving into Wild Oaks Sanctuary. I blink, confused for a moment why I'm here instead of at school. But it all comes rushing back when Becca and Leo run over to me.

"You're safe!" Becca cries as she throws her arms around me. "I freaked out when I found your bike! I knew you were in trouble and convinced the sheriff to search for you."

"Thanks," I say with weary relief. "If the sheriff hadn't showed up when he did, I don't know what would have happened."

Leo frowns at me. "You should never have gotten in that trailer."

"It was the scariest ride of my life!" I glance down

at the scratches on my arms. "But I was so worried about Zed, I had to do something. But what's going to happen to Zed now?"

Becca's mother comes over as I'm asking this. "I'll do what I can to make sure Caleb stays away from him." She pushes back her tangled, dark curls. "I'm ashamed at how badly he fooled me."

"He fooled all of us," Becca says, squeezing her mother's hand.

"Yeah," I agree. "I wouldn't have known what he'd done if his sister hadn't warned me to keep Caleb away from the zorse."

Becca's eyes widen. "You talked to Caleb's sister? When did this happen, and why didn't you tell me?"

"And what happened to the fly mask?" Leo adds.

"Save the inquisition until we're inside the house." Mrs. Morales puts her arm around me. "We'll talk after I make us all hot chocolates."

"Topped with whipped cream?" Leo asks hopefully.

"Smothered in whipped cream," she says with a grin.

Minutes later, I'm sitting cozily between Becca and Leo on the couch, licking whipped cream off my steaming hot chocolate.

After hiding in a trailer, galloping on a zorse,

and riding in a sheriff's car, it feels good to sink into a soft couch surrounded by my friends.

"So talk," Becca says, setting her hot cup on a coaster. "And don't leave out any details. Leo and I want to know everything."

Taking a deep breath, I start with my phone call from Carol Hunter-Bowling.

"I couldn't get through to you," I explain to Becca, "so I rode my bike here as fast as I could. I freaked when I saw the horse trailer leaving. All I could think about was Carol's warning not to leave Caleb with Zed. But Caleb was driving away with the horse trailer, and I didn't see you or your mother. So I climbed into the trailer."

"That was crazy." Becca shakes her head. "You should have just come into the house—that's where Mom and I were. After I loaded Zed in the trailer, I couldn't stop crying and I ran to my room. Mom came after me, and when I saw she was crying too, we cried together. Then we talked."

"A really good talk," Mrs. Morales adds, squeezing her daughter's hand.

"But I should have checked my phone messages." Becca groans. "I'm so sorry, Kelsey. I had no idea you were in trouble. I thought you'd changed your mind about coming to my house and went straight to school. It wasn't until I was riding my bike out of the driveway that I saw a glint in the bushes and found your bike. OMG. I totally freaked."

"She sure did." Mrs. Morales looks at her daughter proudly. "Becca demanded that I call the sheriff. Chad—I mean, Sheriff Fischer—is a good friend, so he rushed right over with his deputy. He suggested we check phone messages—that's when we found out about Caleb. Sheriff Fischer called in an alert and learned there were strange reports about a horse trailer with a glowing orb floating beside it."

"Not an orb—a sunflower," I say, then explain how I hung the sunflower on a whip. "But the flower unraveled."

"Sunflower Mary will give you another one," Becca says. "Especially when she learns her flower helped rescue you and the zorse."

"I owe her a big thank-you and maybe something sparkly," I add, touching the necklace around my neck. "What do you think about making her an honorary Sparkler like me?"

Laughing, Becca agrees it's a great idea.

The doorbell rings.

"Chad," I hear Becca's mother say as she opens the door for the sheriff. "Come on in. Would you like some hot chocolate?"

He shakes his head. "Sounds delicious, but I'm here for business, not pleasure. My deputy is waiting for me outside by the horse trailer. We can't keep a zorse at the station, so we brought him here."

"Zed is back!" Becca cries, then starts for the door.

But her mother calls her back. "Sit down, Becca. It's rude to rush off when we have guests."

I glance over at Becca, expecting her eyes to narrow with resentment. But she just shrugs. "Sorry, Mom. Zed can wait—but not too long."

Mrs. Morales turns to the sheriff. "As you can see, we're delighted to have Zed back."

"He won't be here for long," Sheriff Fischer adds. "I talked to his real owner—not that lowlife cowboy, but the grandmother who is surprising healthy for someone supposedly near death."

"More of Caleb's lies," Becca gripes.

"What did she say?" I ask.

"Plenty. That grandson of hers is a—" he starts to answer but is interrupted by door chimes. "Must be my deputy. I'll get it."

Only it's not the deputy.

A tall woman, probably near forty, with curly reddish-black hair curled into a bun steps into the living room. She's wearing a powder-blue business suit, and even though she's older than she was in the video Caleb showed us, I recognize her.

Carol Hunter-Bowling.

- Chapter 22 -
All That Glitters

It's like a party as our group talks excitedly, sitting around the living room table. Everyone sips hot chocolate except Carol Hunter-Bowling, who prefers herbal tea.

Sheriff Fischer does most of the talking since he's collected all the facts about what happened today. He's a fact collector, I think, like I'm a secret collector.

Carol doesn't say much, nodding occasionally while she listens to the sheriff. She sips her tea and shows no emotion except for a *tap-tap* of her rose-red nails on the armrest.

When Sheriff Fischer finishes talking, he asks Carol if she wants to file a report against her brother.

Carol's forehead furrows. "Will he be arrested?"

"That's up to you and your grandmother. He isn't a kidnapper, so I don't have grounds to detain him. But the truck and horse trailer are registered to your grandmother, so I'm not releasing them to him until I've cleared it with her or her legal representative."

"That would be me," Carol says with a wry smile. "Since Grandma's stroke, I've been taking care of her finances."

"I suspected as much." Sheriff Fischer nods. "Your brother wasn't too happy when we refused him access to the truck and trailer. My deputy allowed him to take his suitcase under close supervision. I told your brother you were on the way, but he wasn't keen on hanging around the station. Last I saw, he was being picked up by a friend."

"He can walk back to Nevada for all I care," Carol says bitterly. "I've overlooked his schemes before, but hurting Domino is unforgivable. It'll be up to Grandma, though, if we file charges against him." She turns to me with a grateful smile. "Thank you so much for helping Domino—or you can call him Zed. I'd like to give you a reward."

When I return lost pets, I'm usually happy to accept a reward for our CCSC treasury. But when she pulls out a checkbook, I shake my head. "I care about Zed too much to accept money for helping him. But it would be nice if Becca could visit Zed."

"Of course she can." Carol's smile includes all of us. "You're all welcome at our ranch. I'll be moving in with Grandma, and I know she'd love to meet you."

"Coolness!" Becca jumps up to hug Carol, who seems a little reserved at first but then returns the hug. "How soon can I visit?"

"Anytime you want. And if the zorse ever needs a new home, it's good to know he has one here." She glances toward the window. "I do wonder, though, how I'm going to drive both my car and the truck trailer home."

"Sorry, I can't help you with that," Sheriff Fischer says as he walks over to the door. "My deputy's waiting outside and we have to leave."

"I'll figure something out, but I won't be able to come back for the truck and trailer until the weekend." She looks at Becca's mother. "If that's all right with you?"

"He can stay as long as you want. He has a home here whenever he needs it." Mrs. Morales touches her chin thoughtfully. "I just had an idea."

"What?" Carol arches her brows.

"I have plenty of experience driving horse trailers. Why not let me drive the trailer back for you? I can drive up on Saturday and get one of my volunteers to follow in his car, and the others can stay here to help run the sanctuary."

Carol's big grin is answer enough.

"I can't wait any longer." Becca jumps up. "Now can I go out and see Zed?"

"I want to see him too," Carol says, heading for the door.

The sheriff, Becca's mom, Leo, and I follow them outside. Becca and Carol rush over to the trailer, so I'm the only one that sees Sheriff Fischer reach out to hold Mrs. Morales's hand—and she doesn't pull away. She smiles at him like she doesn't just have a "thing" for cowboys but for sheriffs too.

Secret thirty-one, I think with a smile.

Becca and Carol are hugging and bonding over Zed love. I notice Leo standing off to the side. He's tilting his head in his "thinking" mode. I call his name repeatedly before he blinks at me.

"Huh?" he murmurs as if coming out of a trance. "Did you say something?"

"Only your name like a dozen times," I tease. "Why so serious? You should be happy that Zed is safe. We found out who hurt him and helped reunite him with his family. Another CCSC mystery solved."

"But not all the mysteries are solved," Leo points out. "Have you forgotten the fly mask?"

"No." I hesitate, not sure how to tell Leo that his new friend Frankie is our top suspect. But it's not a secret I can keep any longer.

So I explain about Becca sneaking back into the drama storage room and finding the ripped paper that she pieced together. "Frankie spied on us," I finish.

"I know," Leo says surprisingly. "He told me."

"He did?" I gasp.

"Yeah. He had dinner at my house last night and confessed he followed me because he couldn't understand why we were sneaking around to-gether. I didn't tell him about our club, just that we shared an interest in helping animals. I showed him Lucky and some of my robots. He showed me photos of costumes and sets he's created." Leo looks straight into my eyes. "I know he didn't take the fly mask."

"But he's the only one who knows about our

clubhouse," I point out. "At first I thought maybe Caleb took the mask, but he had no reason to, since we were going to give it to him anyway. But Frankie may have felt the fly mask belonged to him because it was in his costume box."

"He's innocent," Leo insists.

I wave my hands in frustration. "No one else knows about our clubhouse."

"Actually someone does," a voice comes from behind us. "I do."

I turn to face Mrs. Morales. "You...you know about our club?"

"That old skunk shack," she says with a nod. "I've known since you kids cleaned it up—nice job. I wanted to help with the kittens and was going to offer kitten supplies, but you've managed great without my help."

"If you knew, why didn't you tell us?" I exclaim.

"And spoil your fun? What kind of mom do you think I am?" She chuckles. "Caleb noticed you sneaking up the hill though and thought I should find out what you were up to. But I told him I trust you kids. You're taking wonderful care of the kittens."

"The orange one is mine, but I can't keep it because my apartment doesn't allow pets," I say, sighing. "The black one is Becca's, and she can't keep it because—"

"Because she thinks I won't let her," Becca's mom finishes. "This calls for another mother-daughter talk. And this time I'll tell her I'm glad she has a club and new friends, but I think the kittens should move into our house. We can always find room for more animals."

"That's great!" I jump up to hug her. "Becca is going to be so happy."

"I'll talk to her now," Mrs. Morales says, then turns and goes over to the pasture, where Becca and Carol are leading Zed.

I glance over at Leo, and he's tilting his head again, staring into space.

"Earth to Leo," I say, tapping his shoulder.

He gives a start. "Oh yeah. This proves my point."

"What point?"

"Frankie is innocent," Leo says firmly.

"Huh?" I ask, totally lost by his thought process.

"Mrs. Morales just said Caleb knew about the Skunk Shack. When he told me he wanted the fly mask hidden somewhere safe, he expected us to hide it in the shack. And he was right. So late last night, he went to the shack and took it."

I shake my head. "Why steal something we were going to give to him?"

"That puzzled me too, but I have a theory. Caleb wouldn't want anyone to know he had the mask, since he planned to sell it even though it doesn't belong to him. So he stole it from us before we could give it to him. He might have also worried we'd figure out the mask is valuable. Last night I researched the jewels and determined there's a 78 percent chance the jewels are real."

"But you proved they're fake," I argue.

"The purple ones are paste imitations," he agrees. "But the black stones are chocolate diamonds."

"Chocolate like candy?" I repeat, confused.

"Chocolate diamonds are also called brown diamonds. The stones are common and used to be thought worthless until they became popular in the late 1980s. If you look under bright lighting, they shine inside."

"Even if they are chocolate diamonds, what does it matter?" My shoulders sag in frustration. "Caleb is gone, and we'll never see him or the fly mask again."

"Do *not* assume the worst." Leo abruptly whirls around.

"Where are you going?" I ask.

"To follow an idea."

He walks over to the truck and opens the door. "Not locked," he reports as he steps up into the back. "But if it had been locked, I could have used my new and improved key spider."

He bends over to peer under the driver's seat, then runs his hands along the cracks between the seats.

"Leo, what are you doing?" I ask.

"Looking for—" He checks the glove box, then lets out a sharp whistle. "Found it!"

When he turns back to me, purple paste jewels and chocolate diamonds sparkle from the fly mask.

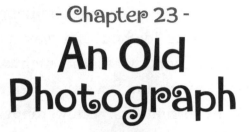

- Chapter 23 -
An Old Photograph

"Are we there yet?" Becca has asked her mother this at least a hundred times, so it's become a joke, and we all laugh.

Becca wiggles in the front seat of the truck beside her mother. Leo and I are in the backseat. The drive to Nevada is long, but we've had a lot to talk about—especially my mother's big news.

I still can't believe it was Mom—not Dad—who found a new job. Mom took the printout with the list of jobs that I gave Dad and applied for one of them. While I was hiding in a horse trailer, Mom was hired to be the new animal control officer. She'll be working full-time with the sheriff's department. That's why Sheriff Fischer knew who she was. And my family won't have to leave Sun Flower.

"Are we there yet?" Becca asks again.

I playfully swat her, although I'm impatient too. We've been driving for hours. It was fun at first, peering out the window as the highway wound through small towns and big cities until it climbed high into the mountains. Snow-topped Sierras beckoned us higher, and twisty miles of forest rose, then fell into high desert hills.

I must have drifted asleep because suddenly I sit up with a start as Mrs. Morales announces, "We're here!"

The Hunters' ranch sits in a valley surrounded by low hills. We drive through a wooden gate, onto a paved road circling up to a brick and fawn-brown colored single-story house with a wraparound wood deck and potted cactuses. A Labrador retriever barks and wags his tail excitedly as he chases after our car.

The front door of the house swings opens. Carol Hunter-Bowling comes out, pushing a wheelchair with a silver-haired woman draped in a bright-red shawl.

"I'm so glad you're here!" Carol says warmly, giving us hugs. "This is my grandmother, Eloise Hunter."

I'm not sure what I expected—maybe a feeble, hunched-over woman who was too frail to speak. Mrs. Hunter's face is lined and she's attached to a breathing tube, but she sits tall in her chair with bright-blue eyes.

"Oh my," she says, pointing at the horse trailer. "Is it really him?"

"Yes," her granddaughter answers.

"My sweet Dom...I can hardly believe it." The old woman stares ahead like she expects the horse trailer to vanish. "I thought he was dead."

"He's very much alive," Becca's mother says.

"I never thought I'd see him again...but here he is." She grips her wheelchair with shaky hands. "Thank you, girls, so much."

"He's a special animal," Becca says softly.

"And he's back...My Domino is home." She wipes a tear from her wrinkled cheek and turns to her daughter. "Take me to him. Please."

"Of course, Mom," Carol replies, looking close to tears too.

When Becca unlatches the trailer and Zed backs out, Mrs. Hunter grips her wheelchair tightly. She pushes herself up, slowly standing.

"Are you sure you can handle walking?" Carol asks.

"Move over and let me see my sweet Domino," the elderly woman says. She takes a shaky step forward, then another. Her blue eyes shine, and for a moment I see past her wrinkles and age spots to the younger woman in the photos.

"Domino...Dom baby...it's really you." She wraps her arm around the zorse. "I've missed you so much."

Zed lowers his head and caresses the old woman with his muzzle. He's not rough or stubborn but lovingly gentle.

"It's so good to hold you again," Mrs. Hunter says. "When I'm stronger, we'll go for a ride."

"Don't forget this," Becca says and reaches into her back pocket.

"Domino's fly mask!" Eloise Hunter cries, clasping the mask to her chest. When her legs buckle, Carol and Becca's mom quickly come to her side and ease her back into the wheelchair. "Thank you, but I'm fine," Eloise says. "I'm just overwhelmed with joy. I never expected to see Domino again, much less the jeweled mask."

"Leo thinks the black stones are chocolate diamonds," I say.

"Clever boy." Eloise Hunter chuckles. "Most people

think the purple stones are the valuable ones, but those are imitation amethysts. My husband had a quirky sense of humor and always made a game of giving me special gifts. When I unwrapped the mask, I was delighted by the sparkly stones. I had no idea they were real until my husband offered to string them into a necklace for me. But I liked seeing them on Domino—and I still do." She hands the fly mask to her daughter, who slips it over Zed's muzzle and fastens it in place. The fake purple jewels sparkle brighter than the valuable black diamonds.

Zed and his fly mask are home.

It's hours before we get back home, and it's almost dark—but not too dark for a quick visit to the Skunk Shack. We're going to pick up the kittens, their bed, and their litter box, and move them into a back room of Becca's house.

And there's something else on the CCSC agenda.

Leo has been mysterious for the last few hours, teasing about a surprise he has for us. No matter how hard I try, I can't pry this secret from him.

All he'll say is that it's in the shack.

As we hike up the hill, Becca and I pester him with more questions.

"It better not be Frankie," Becca warns. "It's bad enough he knows about our shack."

"Not Frankie, and I already told you we can trust him. He promised not to tell anyone about our kittens or the shack."

"Is it another kitten?"

"Nothing alive," Leo says, then hurries ahead to the shack and disappears inside.

When we enter the shack, he's standing by the grandfather clock—not pieces of a broken clock but a full-size, repaired clock taller than us—and it's ticking.

"I fixed the clock!" Leo says proudly. "It will chime on the hour."

I check my watch. "That's in three minutes."

"Coolness," Becca says. "I'm so proud of you!"

"Me too," I add. "Congratulations, Leo."

Cuddling my kitten in my arms, I stand beside my two club mates as we stare at the hands of the clock.

Leo counts down. "Two minutes forty-three seconds...one minute and twenty-two seconds... thirteen seconds...WHAT?"

The small clock hand stops.

"Drats," I say. "Sorry, Leo. Guess it still needs work."

With a determined press of his lips, Leo sorts through his box of tools and picks up a screwdriver. He tugs the corner of the clock face and the glass cover swings open. He pokes the screwdriver into gears below a decorative golden moon. As he tinkers, his elbow bumps the moon, and it swings sideways.

A small piece of paper floats to the floor.

"What's this?" Leo says, reaching down.

Becca and I crowd around him as he holds out the paper.

"A photo," Becca says.

"An old black-and-white photo," I add, peering closer. "The little boy looks like he's having fun riding a huge turtle."

"Not a turtle—a tortoise." Leo flips over the photo and points to tiny handwritten numbers. "According to my calculations, if this is the date the photo was taken, the child would be 106 years old."

"Wow—that's really old," I say.

"He probably died a long time ago," softhearted Becca says with a sigh.

"I'm more interested in the tortoise than the boy."

An excited gleam lights up Leo's face. "A famous Egyptian tortoise lived to be over two hundred years old. If we solve the mystery of who left this photo in the clock, we may find the tortoise too. He might still be alive."

Stay tuned for the next
Curious Cat Spy Club
mystery...

Kelsey the Spy!

Coming soon!

About the Author

At age eleven, Linda Joy Singleton and her best friend, Lori, created their own Curious Cat Spy Club. They even rescued three abandoned kittens. Linda was always writing as a kid—usually about animals and mysteries. She saved many of her stories and she loves to share them with kids when she speaks at schools. She's now the author of over forty books for kids and teens, including YALSA-honored the Seer series and the Dead Girl trilogy. Her first picture book, *Snow Dog, Sand Dog*, was published by Albert Whitman & Company in 2014. She lives with her husband, David, in the northern California foothills on twenty-eight acres surrounded by a menagerie of animals—horses, peacocks, dogs, and (of course) cats. For photos, contests, teacher guides, and more, check out www.LindaJoySingleton.com.